THE GIRL
WHO
CHANGED
THE
WORLD

THE GIRL
WHO
CHANGED
THE
WORLD

Delia Ephron

TICKNOR & FIELDS
New York
1993

Ticknor & Fields
A Houghton Mifflin company, 215 Park Avenue South,
New York, New York 10003.

Manufactured in the United States of America
Book design by Christine Hoffman
The text of this book is set in 12 pt. Itc Garamond Light.
10 9 8 7 6 5 4 3 2 1

Library of Congress Cataloging-in-Publication Data
Ephron, Delia.
The girl who changed the world / by Delia Ephron.
p. cm.
Summary: Fed up with the injustices she suffers at the hands of
her older brother, Violet organizes the younger siblings of the
neighborhood into a formidable army to demand retribution and a
change in the status quo.
ISBN 0–395–66139–0
[1. Brothers and sisters—Fiction.   2. Revenge—Fiction.]
I. Title.
PZ7.E7246Gi   1993
[Fic]—dc20   92–42444   CIP   AC

To Maia Papaya & Anna Banana
and to Eva

THE GIRL
WHO
CHANGED
THE
WORLD

THE YOUNGERS

Violet Sparks

Melissa McFree

Artie Box

Cynthia Ruggles

Davy Brown

Annabel DeMot

THE OLDERS

Simon Sparks

Suzette McFree

Gabriel Box

Bobby Ruggles

Margaret Brown

THE ANIMAL BRIGADE

(All Youngers)

Alfred

Mugs

Ivy

CHAPTER ONE

In which Violet plays the piano and washes fly guts out of her hair

"I hate this dress." Violet couldn't imagine how she'd ever let her mother trick her into wearing a dress, period, much less one with daisies around the bottom. She hadn't been paying attention. She'd been thinking about playing the piano in public. Playing the stupid "Spinning Song" in front of her teacher and her mom and all the other kids who took piano and all their parents. She was thinking about that while her mother slipped the dress over her head and buttoned it. And she was out the door before she realized that, for the first time in months, she was not wearing jeans and a T-shirt. There was an unfamiliar warm breeze wisping around her bare legs.

"This is not me," she told herself over and over as she, her mom, and Simon walked down Ravencrest Drive that Friday evening.

Her piano teacher, Mrs. DeMot, was standing at her front door, shaking everyone's hand. "Hello, Claire. Hello, Simon. Violet, you look beautiful."

"No, ugly," whispered Simon.

Violet jabbed her elbow back, but Simon moved to the side, so she missed him.

"Violet plays so nicely. I bet she won't make one single mistake," gushed Gloria DeMot.

"Bet you do," hissed Simon.

Violet whirled around, but her brother had shot off toward the dining room, where there was a white tablecloth on the table and plates of cookies with vanilla cream filling. Violet watched him as he almost bumped into a lamp and then tripped over a footstool. She heard her mother laugh.

"Simon's grown so fast I don't think he knows where his body is."

"Why did he have to come?" asked Violet.

"Because he's your big brother and we do things as a family."

Her mother was always saying things like that—like "We do things as a family." It was as if there were laws that she'd passed. No one got to vote on them, and Violet was stuck with them.

"Oh, dear." Mrs. DeMot was fanning the air. "Would you all move inside? I have to close this screen door. Those summer flies are coming in."

Violet walked through the hall to the living room. It was exactly the same size and shape as her living room. All the houses in Mountain Terrace had been built at the same time, and they were identical. They were one-story with tile roofs and two-car garages. The living rooms had a fireplace at one end, and, opposite, a large bay window. The only difference between Mrs. DeMot's living room and Violet's was that tonight Mrs. DeMot's husband had moved out all the furniture except the piano and had set up six rows of folding chairs.

"Hi, Violet, can I sit with you?" Annabel DeMot bounced over. She had yellow curls all over her head and a pink ribbon tied in a bow at the top. She reminded Violet of those dolls you squeeze that say, "Mom-my, Mom-my."

"Sure, sit with her, no one else wants to," said Simon. He popped two vanilla cookies in his mouth at once.

"Mind your own business," said Violet.

"Okay, George. Whatever you say, George."

"Stop calling me George."

"Can I?" asked Annabel.

"No." Violet walked over to the front row and sat in the last chair on the end. "I'm going to play perfectly," she said to Simon.

"Wanna bet?" Simon poked his fingernail between his teeth, where a blob of cookie was stuck.

Violet just smiled.

"Simon, Simon." Claire Sparks called and waved from the back row. "Come sit with me."

"So long, George," said Simon, strolling off.

Violet took a deep breath. Peace . . . for at least three minutes. She stretched her legs and looked around. Every other student was younger than her. She was almost eleven and she was playing in a recital with a bunch of babies.

"Do you want me to come with you?" Melissa had asked that morning, when they were hanging out in Violet's bedroom.

"No way. It's boring and, besides, I stink."

"But I'm your best friend, I don't care."

"I don't need you. I'm not nervous." Violet flopped down on the bed, opened a book, and started reading. Melissa knew what that meant: Conversation closed.

Now that the recital was about to start, Violet still wasn't nervous, but she was dreading it. She liked to play the piano for one reason only: her own amusement. She didn't even like the sound of the piano that much, although it was okay. She liked the fact that if she put her fingers on exactly the right keys in exactly the right order, she got back what she expected in exactly the same way every time.

"And now Violet Sparks will start our program with 'Spinning Song.'" Mrs. DeMot clapped, which was a signal. Everyone else joined in.

"I have to go to the bathroom," announced Simon loudly.

"Shush," said Mrs. Sparks. She smiled weakly at the other parents.

"It's through the door next to the kitchen, Simon," said Mrs. DeMot.

Simon was already on his way, since the bathroom was located in the same place that it was in his house.

Violet walked to the piano and sat down. She didn't look at anyone in the audience. She didn't want them to think she cared whether they liked how she played or not. She opened the music book to page 23 and pressed the pages down so they wouldn't turn by accident when she was right in the middle of the song. "Perfectly," she told herself. "I'm going to do it perfectly."

The toilet flushed. A few kids tittered. "Shush," said Mrs. DeMot.

Violet started playing. First the left hand—all it had to do was go back and forth between two keys, dum dum, dum dum. Then the right hand came in. It had all the work. Violet concentrated hard, so hard she barely heard the music she made. She certainly couldn't hear the humongous, hairy fly that flew by her mother's face, buzzing like an old refrigerator. It was fat, very fat, and it moved so slowly it seemed almost to sit in the air as it blocked Violet's mother's view. She waved her hand in front of her face. The fly lumbered off, slowly buzzing its way toward Violet.

Simon came out of the bathroom and stopped. He could see the back of Violet's head bouncing a little, in time to the music. He saw everyone in the audience watching his sister, and his mom smiling, her cheeks red with pleasure. He saw the fly. It circled Violet's head like a plane over an airport. He grinned. He looked around the kitchen, and saw the swatter hanging on a hook by the back door.

Violet played, her eyes almost blurry from staring at the notes on the page. Only three bars left and not one mistake yet. Her right hand jumped up an octave and then back again. "Perfect," Violet said to herself, "completely perfect," as the fly landed on her head. Simon smashed it.

Violet's hands crashed down on the keys.

"Violet?" She dimly heard her mother squeak out her name. She heard the front door slam as her brother raced out. She heard everything, but she heard it as if it were far away. The people in front of her looked funny, like she was seeing them through those amusement park mirrors that pull you out of shape. She saw Mrs. DeMot with her hand in front of her mouth and her eyes like two large O's. Slowly Violet raised her hand and placed it flat on top of her head. Something was there, a pool of something wet and sticky. Slowly she moved her hand back down and held it in front of her eyes. Violet screamed.

The next thing she knew her mother was washing her hand off under the kitchen sink, and gross slimy black fly guts with bits of shiny green stuff were sliding down the drain. "We'll go right home and wash your hair," her mom was saying over and over. "It's just a fly."

Just a fly? Violet was too stunned to answer.

"Of course it was the largest, most disgusting fly I've ever seen," her mother added. "I hope this doesn't give you a trauma." Trauma? Violet couldn't exactly remember what that word meant. She was too busy trying not to cry.

There were two things Violet hadn't done in at least five years. Cry, and throw up. Violet thought everything about throwing up was disgusting—doing it, tasting it, smelling it. Last time she did it, after eating some weird Chinese food, she swore she never would again. Crying was different. She just refused to be the kind of person who cried. That was not how she thought of herself. And this thing with the fly, so gross and so upsetting, could easily make someone, someone with less control than Violet, do both. As soon as Violet's mom had dried Violet's hands with a dishtowel, Violet curled them into fists and held them as tight as she could. It gave her something to concentrate on so not a single tear could sneak out her eyes, but still four did.

"Do you want to leave by the back door?" her mother asked.

"No," said Violet. Before she had time to lose her nerve, she walked straight out of the kitchen, through the living room, past all the kids and parents sitting in the folding chairs, to Mrs. DeMot's front door. She didn't look left or right. She just marched to the door and out. A few kids watched with their hands over their mouths so they wouldn't laugh, but mostly everyone politely looked the other way.

As soon as she was outside, she bolted. She ran up the street to her house and raced inside to the bathroom. She turned on the water full blast, and stuck her head under the faucet. She realized that her heart was jumping like popcorn in a microwave. She turned the water off, grabbed a towel, and rubbed her hair really hard. She examined the towel for fly guts, then went across the hall to her room and slammed the door.

"Violet? Violet?"

"What?" Violet did not open the door.

"Do you want me to help you wash your hair?"

"I already did it."

"Open the door, please."

Violet slowly turned the doorknob. She didn't open the door, however- -she just let it swing back a little. Mrs. Sparks had Simon with her. She pushed him into Violet's bedroom.

Simon's hands were shoved down into his jean pockets and his head was cocked to the side. "I'm sorry," he mumbled. He was biting his lip. Violet couldn't tell whether he was trying not to laugh or was just using his teeth to hold onto his lips because he didn't want to say the words.

"Say it louder," said Mrs. Sparks.

"I'm sorry."

"That's better."

Simon shuffled out. As soon as he was out of sight, he stuck his hand up behind their mom's head so Violet had a clear view of it. His fingers were crossed.

"He's not having any television for a week," said Mrs. Sparks.

"That's all? He swats a fly on my head in public and that's all you're doing to him?"

Her mother sighed.

"That's not fair!"

Her mother sighed again.

Violet hated it when her mother sighed. She had never sighed at all before Violet's dad left a year ago, and now it felt like she did nothing but sigh. Sometimes she sighed in the living room while she was reading a magazine. Sometimes she sighed at the kitchen table in the mornings, her coffee mug cupped in her hands and pressed against her cheek.

"What do you expect me to do, Violet?" Her mother sighed again.

"Nothing. Forget it. Just forget it." Violet closed her bedroom door.

"Violet, don't be so angry."

"Sure, right." Violet unbuttoned her dress, pulled it over her head, and threw it. She yanked open a drawer and yanked out a big T-shirt, one she liked to sleep in. She pulled it on. She sat down at the edge of her bed with her feet flat on the floor and looked straight ahead at absolutely nothing. Her head was still feeling fuzzy from the surprise of it all. She kept really still, not moving even her pinkie. Her head started to clear.

Did she want to read or write? These were Violet's favorite things—to write in her diary and read stories.

True stories. Violet liked only things that really happened.

"Don't you ever pretend?" Melissa had asked when Violet first moved in across the street.

"Never," said Violet.

"How come?"

"It's for babies."

"But it's not."

"I think so."

Violet shuffled through a few books in a stack next to her bed. *Madame Curie, Scientist; Abraham Lincoln, the Man from Springfield; Elizabeth Blackwell, Woman Doctor.* Nothing appealed to her. She took the little key off the gold chain around her neck and unlocked her diary, which she kept stashed under her pillow. She sat down at her desk and opened the diary to the date, July 12. There, on the page, on the blank page waiting for her own private thoughts, were two words: HI, GEORGE.

Violet froze.

Minutes went by, then a half hour. Then, an hour.

Eventually Violet turned out the light, took the diary over to her bed, and lay down on her side with the diary open next to her. The moon shone in the window, making the page even whiter, almost glowing white. Simon's black printing popped off it like neon. If Violet slept, she didn't know it.

Eventually the sun peeked out over the horizon. Violet got up and took a shower, washing her hair again to make sure no stray fly legs were left. She dried it, then brushed it even though it wasn't necessary. Violet's hair was short. It stood up in curls all over her head. Hair with a mind of its own, she called it.

At exactly eight-thirty, she went into the hall, picked up the telephone, carried it back into her bedroom, and closed the door.

Melissa's squeaky voice answered after the first ring.

"It's me," said Violet.

"Violet, guess what? They're still fighting. All night they were arguing about whether to name her Christine or Ingrid after some movie star my mom liked when she was ten. It wasn't so bad when the kid was a week old. But it's six months now. I have a baby sister who's six months old and doesn't have a name. That is so embarrassing."

Dead silence.

"Violet? Violet, was the concert okay?"

"Meet me outside this second."

CHAPTER TWO

In which Violet declares war and Melissa almost has a cow

Violet ran out the front door, then stopped short. Simon was shooting baskets in the driveway.

"Buzz, buzz, buzz." Simon laughed, then tripped and dribbled the basketball on his foot.

"Simon, are you okay, did you hurt yourself?" asked Melissa, who was crossing the street from her house to Violet's. She was wearing her usual outfit: big baggy shorts with a T-shirt, and a baseball cap with the brim turned around to the back.

"Nah, no problem," said Simon, shooting a basket for Melissa to admire. "Good shot," she called as Violet yanked her by the shirt and started walking quickly down the block.

"Traitor," hissed Violet. "Traitor of a traitor."

"Who, me? What's going on?" Melissa hurried after her. "Violet, stop, please. What happened?"

Violet waited until they had turned the corner and her house was out of sight. She looked around suspiciously. There was only one man on the street and he was busy watering his flowers. She sat down cross-legged on the sidewalk. Melissa immediately did, too, because that was how she and Violet had all their most serious talks. Then Violet told her about the fly, about the black and green guts oozing in her hair.

"That's so sad," said Melissa when Violet had finished. "Flies feel. Everything feels."

"The fly's not the point." Violet threw up her hands. "He murdered it on my head."

"In public," added Melissa, making an awful face at the thought. "What did your mom do?"

"No TV for a week," said Violet.

"A whole week?"

"That's nothing! This has gone far enough."

"What has?"

"Everything!" Violet jumped up and started walking again. Melissa scrambled up after her.

"Do you know who Joan of Arc was?"

"Wasn't she French?" asked Melissa.

"She led the French army when she was seventeen. They did whatever she said."

"That's three years older than Suzette," said Melissa. "Imagine Suzette leading an army. Did you have breakfast? I'm starved."

"Whatever," said Violet.

They walked to the corner, then down to the bottom of the hill, where the houses ended and there was a traffic light. Across the street was the Mountain Terrace mini-mall, which had a bunch of stores, including a deli, and an all-natural cosmetics shop where Melissa's sister Suzette spent all her allowance.

"The light's green," said Melissa. "Are you looking where you're going?"

"My eyes are staring at my heart. Today I see only what I feel."

"Wow!" said Melissa. "That's amazing."

"Dog biscuits," said Violet. Her eyes narrowed to slits.

Melissa instantly knew what she meant. Violet had once eaten two round dog biscuits with glue in the center because Simon had convinced her it was a new kind of Oreo. They walked into the deli.

Antonia Box was behind the counter, slicing salami. She was large and soft like a pillow. She always wore an apron, which was just a big white cloth wound around her waist and tied with string. Her black hair was pulled straight back over her ears into a bun, and, with her black top and that big white bottom, she reminded Violet of a fancy saltshaker. "Why if it isn't Violetta and Melissina! Get over here this instant." She hugged them both at the same time, then waved her hand in front of her face as if the experience had been exhausting. "Arturo," she boomed, "your friends are here."

Artie stuck his head out of the back room of the deli. Immediately Violet and Melissa were hit with a blast of rock music. "Arturo, please, turn that music down, it is simply poison."

"It certainly is," said Gabriel, who was scooping balls of fresh mozzarella from a bowl into a metal tray. "It's offensive. Like putting vinegar in our dear mother's lasagna."

Gabriel beamed at his mother. He had perfect, very white teeth, and when he smiled, both the top and bottom row showed.

"Listen to your big brother, Arturo."

"My name is Artie," said Artie, scowling. "Want to listen to some hot music?" he asked Violet and Melissa. "Come on back."

"We can't," said Melissa. "We're just getting something to eat, and then Violet has to baby-sit. She always baby-sits on Saturday morning, remember?"

"What can I get you for breakfast, my sweet peppers?" said Antonia Box.

"Lizards," said Violet.

"I'm fresh out of lizards." Antonia Box chuckled.

"A fried-egg sandwich," said Melissa quickly. She knew Violet wasn't making a joke. Violet was thinking about the time she'd gotten into bed and found it crawling with Simon's blue-bellied lizards.

"I'm going to practice now," said Gabriel.

"Oh, you are a gift from heaven, a precious gift." Antonia Box blew a kiss skyward, as if to thank the angels, then she cracked an egg onto the sizzling griddle. "Arturo, someday you'll practice your violin two hours a day just like Gabriel. Just like my precious Gabriel."

"No way," said Artie, disappearing into the back room and slamming the door.

"Right on," said Violet suddenly.

Antonia Box peered down over the counter at Violet. "What did you say?"

"Nothing," said Violet sweetly. "I didn't say anything, Mrs. Box. Thank you for the sandwich."

Mrs. Box wrapped it up in foil and handed it over. Violet paid Mr. Box, who always sat at the cash register and never said a single word.

Violet and Melissa hurried up the street to Davy Brown's house. "Do you know why Joan of Arc won every battle?" Violet asked.

"What do you mean, she won? Didn't she get burned at the stake?"

"That was later. Forget that. She won because she had faith."

"In what? God? Do you want half of this or what?" Melissa took a huge bite out of the sandwich. There was egg all around her mouth.

"In God. But it doesn't have to be God. It could be faith in yourself or in your cause. Because it's right and just."

A blob of yolk dropped on Melissa's shirt. "Hey, look, I'm a painting," Melissa giggled.

Violet didn't even glance at her. "Remember the wolf." She spoke in a low, ghostly voice.

"Yeah, I remember." Simon had told Violet there was a wolf loose in Mountain Terrace. It had escaped from the zoo, he'd said, and followed the freeway up from Los Angeles.

"Simon hid in my closet," said Violet. "He waited until I was sound asleep, and he howled. I thought I was going to be eaten." Violet's shoulders gave the slightest shudder.

"Maybe you should give him a lifetime of the silent treatment," said Melissa. "It never really lasts. I usually forget to keep it up after a day, but if anyone can do it, it's you."

"No, something bigger."

"Bigger?" Melissa dabbed at the yolk on her shirt with a napkin and managed to smear it some more.

"Something gigantic. Something cosmic."

"What?"

"War," said Violet. She knocked on Davy's door.

Violet left Melissa standing on the doorstep. Her egg sandwich was in one hand, and her mouth was hanging open like an empty garage waiting for a car to drive in and park.

"Hi, Davy," said Violet.

"Who's talking?" He was wearing a huge fire helmet that covered his eyes.

"It's me." Violet tipped his hat back. Davy smiled. Melissa came in slowly. "Don't scare me. I almost had a cow. You're kidding, right?"

"Kidding about what?" asked Davy.

"Nothing," said Melissa. "I have to whisper something to Violet, Davy, but it's not about you." Melissa cupped her hand around her mouth so only Violet could hear. "Do you really want to declare war on your very own brother?"

"No," said Violet.

"I didn't think so."

"It's war on all of them."

"What? Davy, she shouldn't be baby-sitting for you. She's completely lost her marbles."

"I have marbles," said Davy. "Want my marbles,

Violet?" He reached into the pocket of his overalls and pulled some out. They were grimy and sticky. "No thanks." Violet put her face close to Melissa's. "We're going to war against my older brother and your older sister. All the youngers against all the olders."

"What's an older?" Davy asked.

"Why if it isn't Violet Dixie Sparks and Melissa Lauren McFree." Davy's sister, Margaret, was standing in the doorway. She was wearing a pink leotard and a pink headband that pulled her red hair straight back and made her round eyes look like they were popping out of her head. "Did you know that when it's three o'clock in the afternoon in Mountain Terrace, it's two o'clock in the morning in Moscow and midnight in Budapest? Davy can't even tell time." Margaret made three twirls and came to a stop in third position.

"*That's* an older, Davy," said Violet.

"I could tell time at four years eight months, and I could read my very own thermometer at two years six months. Davy doesn't even know when he's sick."

"I'm a dodo," said Davy.

"You said it, I didn't." Margaret did a plié.

"No you're not, you're only six," said Violet.

"Six forever," said Margaret. "Well, ta-ta girls, you

were late getting here and now I'm almost late for my ballet lesson." She arranged her toe shoes, which were tied together, over her shoulder and she sashayed out.

"My sister's not as bad as that," said Melissa. "Besides I——," she hesitated, "——I love her."

"You what?" Violet squawked.

"Well, what I mean is," Melissa was tripping over her words. "I mean, like you hate Simon, right, but you sort of love him anyway because he's your brother."

"No way!"

"Do you love me?" asked Davy. Violet patted him on the head.

"I can't go to war, I just can't." Melissa threw herself in a chair.

"Why not?"

"I rescue birds when they fall out of trees."

"Who doesn't?"

"Once when my dad put a worm on a fishing hook, I threw up. I never even blow on ladybugs to make a wish in case I might hurt them——," Melissa stopped because Violet had turned her back.

She moved around to Violet's front. "Don't be mad, okay?" Violet made another half turn away. "Oh, Violet." Melissa's voice sounded like it needed a nap.

Violet spun around. "Are you in or out? That's all
I want to know."

"That's all?"

"Yes."

"Then I guess I'm . . . ," Melissa paused. "Out."

CHAPTER THREE

In which Violet is stuck with idiotic Annabel, and Melissa gets the works

Violet took the silverware out of the drawer and set the table the way she always did—very precisely. One fork, one knife, one spoon for each, perfectly straight. She was furious. Why didn't Melissa realize what it was like to have someone who was always picking on you? Melissa's sister was totally obnoxious. Suzette was a snob from hell. What was the matter with Melissa anyway? And what was the matter with this fork, which for some reason spun sideways? She banged it down on the table.

"Ooh, George has a temper," said Simon, skateboarding in.

"No skateboarding in the house," said Mrs. Sparks. She tapped a glass with a knife so it made a ping. "Family hour."

Family hour! This was another new development

since their dad left. Claire Sparks insisted that they all get together every evening to discuss their day. It always started in the kitchen while she was getting dinner and ended up at the table while they ate.

"So who goes first?" asked Mrs. Sparks, taking baked potatoes out of the microwave.

"Me, Simon the great." He beat his chest like Tarzan and howled.

Claire Sparks smiled. She took a roast chicken out of a special keep-hot bag and put it on a platter. Claire Sparks bought almost all their food already prepared, but she made sure they used cloth napkins. "That means it's like a home-cooked meal," she said at least once a week. They all sat down.

Simon speared the entire chicken and put it on his plate. "Just kidding, ha-ha." He put the chicken back. "Me and Bobby had a great day," he said. "Like we walked to the corner, okay, and then Bobby goes, 'Hey, you hungry?' and I go, 'No, I'm Simon.' " Simon snorted. Mrs. Sparks laughed. Violet couldn't believe it. That joke was older than America.

Simon droned on about how he and Bobby went to the International House of Pancakes—Simon called it the I-Hop—and had coffee. "Decaf, I hope," said Mrs. Sparks. And how the waitress thought they were seventeen. On and on he droned, which normally drove Violet crazy. Simon thought every single thing that happened, every thought that ran through his tiny brain, was fascinating. He never left anything out. Violet was sure that if they sold tape recordings of him at the drugstore, people could use them for sleeping pills. Get into bed, turn on Simon, and in two seconds you'd be dead to the world. But today Violet was going to take advantage of Simon's droning. Today, while Simon droned, Violet prepared for battle.

She practiced looking at him with what she imagined was a friendly face, though not real smiley, while she thought horrible thoughts about him. "Pea-brained warthog," she thought, while her eyes said, "Angel pie." "Ugly fart-face," she thought, while her eyes said, "Handsome devil." Sitting there looking sweetly at Simon, Violet invented her first rule of war: Never let the enemy know what's coming.

"Aren't you hungry?" said Mrs. Sparks. Violet hadn't touched her food.

"I'm fine," said Violet. The doorbell rang. She jumped up.

She was sure it was Melissa coming to say that Violet was right, she could never let her down, she'd do anything Violet asked. Violet was surprised it had taken Melissa all day to figure this out, but she'd forgive her. Violet thought of herself as someone who was very fair. Still, she didn't rush. If she was going to be a general, she had to act like one. She'd never heard of a general racing to the door to greet his best friend. The bell rang again. Violet stood tall and wiped every bit of eagerness off her face. She opened the door.

"Want to play?" said Annabel DeMot.

Violet's shoulders sagged. "I'm eating dinner."

"Who's there?" yelled Mrs. Sparks.

"It's me, Annabel." Annabel headed straight for the dining room. "Hi, Mrs. Sparks. Ooh, chicken, my favorite."

"Would you like a piece?"

"A wing, please." Annabel sat in a chair and started swinging her heels against the chair frame. "Hi, Simon."

"Hey," said Simon.

"*Hey*? Is that the same as hi?" Annabel looked confused.

Violet took a big bite of chicken so Simon couldn't see her smile.

"Are you best friends with George?" asked Simon.

"Who?"

"Vi-o-let." He pronounced every single syllable and wiggled his shoulders in time.

"Could I be?" Annabel looked lovingly at Violet, who took another bite of chicken. Never let the enemy know what's coming, never let the enemy know what's coming.

"You're like just the right age for her, aren't you? Like about seven." Simon flexed the muscles in his arms and admired them.

"I'm seven and three-quarters," said Annabel, happily crunching the wing.

"That's enough, Simon," said Claire Sparks. "We all get along here, don't we?"

"Come on, Annabel. Let's go to my room." Violet took her plate to the kitchen, rinsed it, and put it in the dishwasher.

"Neat-o." Annabel slid off her chair. "Thanks, Mrs. Sparks." She ran down the hall after Violet.

Violet quickly closed the door behind them. "Do you want to be in my army?"

"Oh, that'll be so fun." Annabel gave Violet a squeeze.

"No hugging. I hate hugging." Violet closed her eyes so she wouldn't scream. She couldn't believe that Melissa had deserted her. She couldn't believe that Melissa had left her stuck with Annabel DeMot, who said totally idiotic things like "so fun."

"Let's pretend we're soldiers," said Annabel.

"Not pretend."

Annabel thought a second. "Then what?"

"Real."

"I'll have to ask my mom."

"No," said Violet.

Annabel looked confused. Her tongue snaked out between her lips and took up a position at the corner of her mouth.

"We're going to fight all the older brothers and sisters."

"Oh, I've always wanted an older sister just like you. Will you be my older sister?"

"Older brothers and sisters are hounds from hell."

"They are? What about younger brothers and sisters?" asked Annabel, who was an only child.

"Forget it," said Violet. "Just forget it. It's time for you to go."

"But I just got here. Can't I be in the army? I won't ask my mom."

"No." Violet waved her arms, shooing Annabel out the door and down the hall. Annabel almost tripped over her own feet trying to move fast enough.

"Are you leaving so soon?" Claire Sparks looked up from the seed catalogue she was reading.

"Yes," said Violet. "She has homework."

"In the summer?"

Violet opened the door. "Bye, Annabel." Before Annabel could protest, Violet pushed her out and closed the door.

"Homework in the summer? That doesn't make any sense." Claire Sparks shook her head.

Second rule of war, thought Violet, Learn to tell better lies.

Across the street at Melissa's, dinner was late. It was always late, thought Melissa, as she banged out the screen door and went into the back yard. Her stomach was upset—it felt like there was a rock inside it. She kept remembering Violet's stony face when Melissa had said, "But can't we be best friends anyway?"

Melissa sat on the swing and drifted back and forth, dragging the toe of her shoe in the grass. Through the living room window she could see her dad on the couch watching baseball, her little brother Max, lying on his stomach, playing a pocket video game. She could hear Suzette on the telephone with her boyfriend, "Ooh, Jockie, ooh, ooh." Melissa remembered that Violet called it squealtalk. Remembering made Melissa's stomach more upset. Violet always had the best names for things.

"Dinner is ready," her mother called. "Melissa, are you coming?"

As Melissa sat down, everyone in the family was grabbing for plates and forks, which were in a pile in the center of the table. The baby was drooped over her mother's shoulder. Her mom burped it as she passed around the macaroni and cheese.

"Guess what, everyone?" announced Suzette.

"What?" asked Mrs. McFree.

"I'm in charge of decorations for the big dance."

Suzette, whose blond hair was wavy—not straight like Melissa's—put her head down and tossed her hair forward. Then she threw her head up and tossed her hair back. She did this a lot for emphasis. "Know what the theme is?"—toss forward, toss backward— "Hair through the ages. I picked it because teenagers love hair. Besides, it's very summer."

"What's summer about it?" asked Melissa.

"If you don't get it, I'm not telling you. Jock is going as a hippie."

"What's that?"

"Oh, these guys in olden times who had long hair and gave away flowers. And I'm going as—"

"My hair's long," piped up Max, who hadn't had a haircut since the baby was born and whose bangs were now down to his eyes.

"Squelch it, shrimp, I'm talking," said Suzette.

"He's not a shrimp," said Melissa.

"Suzette, knock it off," said her father.

"Well, it's my dance and I'm planning it." Suzette's

voice got very high, like there was a sob inside it. "We weren't talking about his hair, were we?"

"No, we weren't," said her mom.

Melissa's parents glared at each other. Melissa pretended to look very intently at her fork.

"Yikes, the phone." Suzette jumped up, knocking her chair backward, and tore out. They heard a happy screech. "Jockikins."

Jockikins? Melissa wasn't sure if it was hearing that sickening nickname or if she was just feeling worse about Violet, but she thought she might faint. Still, what Violet wanted to do was wrong. "Wrong," Melissa said aloud.

"What's wrong?" her dad asked.

"Nothing."

"You sure?"

"I'm sure." She managed a feeble smile.

After dinner, she worked on the dollhouse she was building. She was having a difficult time keeping the chimney perched at the very top of the roof while she drove in the nail, but she was much happier. "Hammering takes your mind off trouble," Melissa's grandmother had told her when she gave Melissa the tool kit for her last birthday. Melissa's grandmother knew, because she had built her entire house from scratch. That's how she had described it—like her house was a batch of cookies that hadn't been made from a mix.

"Hey, Melissa."

"What?" Melissa stopped hammering. Suzette was calling from down the hall.

"Want to see what I'm doing?"

"Me?"

"Of course you."

Melissa went down the hall, skipping a little because she was pleased. Suzette seldom invited her to her bedroom. See, she thought, older sisters could be nice sometimes. Violet only had an older brother, so she probably didn't know.

"What do you think?" asked Suzette. She had piled up her hair so it looked like seventeen doughnuts were stacked on her head. Around each doughnut, like it was a package, was a narrow red ribbon tied in a bow.

"Is that all you?"

"Get real, of course not. I've stuffed little balls of paper under my hair. It's quite an invention."

Melissa patted Suzette's head. She could hear the paper squishing underneath. "That's neat."

"I'm going to the dance as Marie Antoinette. She was a French queen who spent too much money and got her head chopped off. Toss your hair," she said suddenly.

Melissa flipped her head forward, then up, but her hair, straight and wispy, hung limply in exactly the same place.

"Pathetic, no offense," said Suzette, picking up a couple of strands of Melissa's light brown hair and dropping them. "Would you like me to give you the works?"

"Huh?"

"Madame Suzette at your service." Suzette whipped out her desk chair and extended her arm, gesturing for Melissa to sit.

"Thank you, Madame," Melissa giggled. She sat down and wiggled back in the chair until she was cozy and comfortable.

Suzette cocked her head to one side and studied Melissa. She cocked her head to the other side and studied some more. Melissa felt uncomfortable and flattered all at once.

"Too bad about your eyes," said Suzette finally.

"What's wrong with them?"

"So small. Like little gray buttons."

Buttons? Melissa looked in the mirror. She'd never noticed that.

"Oh, well, that's life. Put your head down and keep those little buttons closed. I'll take care of them too."

Melissa could feel Suzette combing her hair backward in little short strokes. "Okay," said Suzette, "head up." She attached rubber bands here and there, and then, after rummaging through some jars on the bureau, drew little lines on Melissa's eyes. Suzette hummed to herself, and Melissa, with her eyes closed, got this comfy, drowsy feeling you get when someone is looking after you.

"Now stand up." Melissa stood and Suzette turned her to the mirror. "Presto, magico, Madame Suzette is finished."

Melissa looked. Her hair was tied in little knots all over her head except on top, where it shot straight up like a geyser. Her eyes were painted green, blue, and silver. "I look like . . . like a freak," she burst out.

"You always look like a freak," giggled Suzette. "Now you look like a freakette. Hey, Mom," she called, "Come see Melissa."

"No!" Melissa pulled out the rubber bands and threw them. She ran into her room and slammed the door.

Her head hurt. Her tears, all mixed up with the makeup, made little rainbow rivers down her cheeks. She looked like an Indian in runny war paint. Melissa grabbed her pillow and rubbed it over her face, trying to get the stuff off, then she threw herself on the bed. "I don't have little gray buttons. I don't, I don't, I don't."

There was a knock. Melissa didn't answer. "Melissa, it's me, Suzette.

"Melissa, may I come in? Please, pretty please, pretty please with sugar on top and a cherry? I'm coming in." Suzette threw open the door. Melissa sat up.

Suzette had her hands on her hips, and her Marie Antoinette hairdo was tilting like the Tower of Pisa. "You didn't look that weird."

Melissa didn't say anything.

"Jock thinks you're cute."

"He does?"

"No, but maybe he would if you'd get rid of that frizzball friend, Violet—"

"She's not a frizzball."

"Are you kidding? With that hair, she's frizz-hell, and it's catching."

"Stop it," screamed Melissa. "She's my best friend. And she's the best, best friend—YOU'LL BE SORRY." Melissa ran past her, grabbed the phone off the hall table, and locked herself in the bathroom.

Violet had drawn a map of Mountain Terrace. She'd put a big *X* on Ravencrest Drive where her house was, and then a star at the DeMots'. The fly may have died, but the war has begun, thought Violet.

She paused to admire herself for thinking that up. "The fly may have died, but the war has begun." She took another sheet of paper and wrote it down. She was trying to get into the swing of being a general, and she knew from her books that they sometimes said memorable things, like Don't shoot until you see the whites of their eyes. If she kept a record of her important sayings, they, too, could end up in history books.

Violet had sharpened all her colored pencils and lined them up in a row. She'd drawn the map in black, the X's in red, and the stars in green. Her first two rules of combat—(1) Never let the enemy know what's coming, and (2) Learn to tell better lies—were in yellow. Her famous sayings, of which there was only one right now, were in royal blue. "Royal blue is definitely my color," thought Violet. The phone rang.

"Violet Sparks here," said Violet, trying to talk in a military way.

"I'm on your team," said Melissa passionately.

"Not team, army," said Violet. "We start tomorrow."

"Wait a minute."

"What?"

"No guns, okay?"

"Oh, please," said Violet. "I have something much more interesting in mind."

CHAPTER FOUR

In which Violet rallies the troops, and Annabel almost dies of curtain suffocation

Violet was picking the raisins out of her cereal and putting them on a napkin.

"What are you doing today?" asked her mom, sitting down at the breakfast table with a cup of coffee.

"Melissa and I are going to the center."

"Why don't you swim? Get some exercise, have fun."

Violet rolled her eyes.

"What's wrong with swimming? You used to love to dive for pennies."

"Claire, I'm almost eleven."

Her mother put her cup down. "Is this something new?"

"What?" Violet asked innocently.

"Calling me Claire."

"Things are changing," said Violet. Then she wondered whether that should go on her famous sayings sheet. No, she decided immediately, it doesn't make the cut. She smiled to herself. *Make the cut* was an expression she'd heard from Melissa's sister when she'd tried out for cheerleader. "I made the cut," Suzette had screamed while she jumped up and down.

"What things exactly are changing?" asked her mom, looking at her very seriously.

"Have you ever noticed how soggy raisin bran gets?" said Violet. "It's like wet sawdust. Probably it was invented for horses, but they decided to sell it to people."

"Don't change the subject."

"What subject?" Violet put her bowl in the sink. "I'll be back later."

At the top of the hill, above the houses, was the Mountain Terrace Community Center. In addition to a swimming pool, it had two tennis courts, an exercise gym, and several meeting rooms. Melissa and Violet went down the hall to the big bulletin board, where all the coming events were announced. There was a poster for the summer dance. PARTY-TIME IS JULY 27, it said. CELEBRATE HAIR THROUGH THE AGES. On a table next to the board were a stack of ballots so teenagers could vote for the queen of the dance.

"Don't forget that date," said Violet, looking at the poster.

"Why? We can't go. We're not old enough."

"That's the day the war starts. On July 27, some kids will be dancing and some—," Violet paused dramatically, then decided not to finish the sentence.

She took down the reserve-a-room sheet, which was tacked to the bulletin board, and reserved the largest room, the one with a stage and a hundred folding chairs. "We'll hold our first rally right here, under their big fat older-brother-and-sister noses," she said to Melissa as she wrote her name and the day, Wednesday. For the activity, she put, "Private club, members only."

"Stick 'em up."

Violet's hands shot into the air. She dropped the sign-up sheet, which floated slowly to the ground.

"Oh my goodness, did I scare you?"

Violet recognized the weaselly voice and whipped around. Simon and his best friend, Bobby Ruggles, pointed their index fingers at her. "Bang, bang, you're dead," said Simon. They cracked up.

Bobby picked up the piece of paper. "What's this?" Simon looked.

Violet crossed her arms casually and tried to look superior. Keep calm no matter what, she told herself, and realized instantly it was her third rule of war.

"Ooh-la-la, a private club." Simon punched Bobby in the arm. "Say, 'How private?'"

"How private?" said Bobby.

"So private no one goes, except to the bathroom!" They howled with laughter.

"Grossiola," shrieked Bobby.

"Last one in the pool's a pig from Peru like George." Simon dropped his skateboard on the floor, hopped on, and skateboarded out.

Melissa's legs went as soft and wiggly as cooked spaghetti. She sank to the floor. "Suppose they figured out . . . ?"

"They wouldn't," said Violet. "They're too dumb."

"Who's dumb, me?" asked Davy, who had walked into the center as Simon and Bobby had glided out.

"Of course not," said Violet. "Do you remember what you have to do?"

Davy stood there staring at his shoes. "Recruit," he said finally. "What's that?"

"No offense, but I think he may be hopeless," whispered Melissa.

Violet ignored her. "You have to bring new members to the meeting on Wednesday. That's two days from now. As many youngers as you can find."

"I can't," said Davy.

"Can," said Violet. "Can, can, can."

* * *

On Wednesday afternoon, Violet stood on the stage behind the curtain. Was anyone coming? She'd spent Monday and Tuesday at the supermarket in aisle four, behind the Oreos. Whenever she heard "It's not fair, he got to push the cart last week," she'd peek around and there'd be a mom or dad with two kids. The older one was usually pushing the cart and acting like he was practically a chauffeur or something. She slipped a little piece of folded-up paper into each younger's hand. It said:

CONFIDENTIAL
READ AND DESTROY!
If your older brother or sister makes you sick, you must come to a meeting Wednesday at 2:00 P.M. in room 101 of the community center.

Violet had passed out so many notes she lost count. Someone had to come. Someone. Her palms were wet. She wiped them off on her jeans.

I'll just peek out the window, and if no one's there, fine, thought Violet. She stood on her tiptoes so her eyes were just high enough to see out. "Oh my gosh!"

Kids, practically thirty, were headed her way. On bicycles, skateboards, roller skates. It's not possible, she thought. It is possible! She heard the door banging. "Is this room 101?" "What room is this?" And Melissa shouting, "Come on in, you're in the right place."

Melissa had a seat in front, next to Cynthia Ruggles, whose brother Bobby was Simon's best friend. Cynthia had long braids and, while they waited for everyone to get seated, she twirled one like a lasso. "I brought my book in case it gets boring," said Cynthia.

"What book?" asked Melissa.

"*Sixty Gruesome Ways to Die.*"

"Sixty what? Where'd you get that?"

"Out of the library. Want to hear my favorite, 'Number 12, Death by Red Ants?' "

"No, not now," said Melissa. "Where do you think Artie is?" She twisted around to look back at the door.

"Beats me. Maybe he didn't want to come?"

"Of course he does. Maybe his mom made him work at the deli. Maybe Gabriel put him in chains and forced him to play a violin duet." Melissa kept her eyes glued to the door. "Where is he?"

Behind the curtain, Violet wiped her sweaty hands one more time, snapped her shoulders back, and stepped out. "Is everyone here?" she asked in a loud, clear voice. "At exactly two o'clock the doors will be locked and no one else will be permitted to enter."

Everyone watched the wall clock. It was 1:59. As the second hand went around, they counted down . . . fifty-nine, fifty-eight, fifty-seven . . . And, finally, five, four, three, two . . . The door jiggled, then slowly opened. "Hurrah, it's Artie!" Melissa sat back, relieved. "Huh?" She jerked up.

In came Davy Brown. Sitting on his head, on top of his fire helmet, was a parrot, and following him were a Siamese cat and a gray dog with skinny short legs and a fat little body.

Melissa jumped up. "No animals allowed."

"But I . . . ," Davy stopped.

"Hey, talk louder, we can't hear," someone yelled.

"I recruited them." Davy's voice trembled. "Wasn't I supposed to?" His nose was runny. He wiped it with the back of his hand.

"A dog? A parrot?" Melissa collapsed in her chair. Cynthia hooted.

"Are they youngers?" Violet's voice boomed out.

"Yes," said Davy. His voice got firmer now that he was speaking to Violet. "This is Ivy." He picked up the cat. "Moonglow, her older sister, always hogs their owner's lap. She never gets petted." Davy wiped his nose again, and sniffed really loudly.

"Turn off your nose, it's dripping," giggled Melissa.

"This is Mugs," he pointed to the dog. "Scuffy, his

older brother, takes his bone away, and then chews it right in front of him." Melissa stopped giggling, that was so mean.

"I'm Alfred, I'm Alfred, I'm Alfred," said the parrot.

"Alfred's sister, Flo, won't let him on the perch. And even worse. Do you want to know what's even worse, Violet?" said Davy.

"What?"

"Well, you see, everyone thinks Alfred and Flo are lovebirds and they make Alfred go 'Cootchy coo' to Flo after she's been mean to him. It's hu—, hu—"

"Humiliating?" Violet asked gently.

"Yes." Davy was exhausted. He tipped his helmet up and wiped off his forehead. "Did I do bad, Violet?"

"Not bad. Good."

"Great," shouted Melissa.

Cynthia raised her hand.

"Yes?" said Violet.

"The kid's got a parrot on his head. What if it poops?"

"That's why he's wearing a helmet. Now can we begin?"

Violet planted her feet slightly apart. Her dark curly hair framed her face like a halo, and her large brown eyes gazed solemnly out. Violet knew her eyes were powerful. She sometimes stood in front of a mirror and tried to see how long she could go without blinking. "Other people can hold their breath," she had said to Melissa. "I can hold my eyes."

As Violet stared, the audience became uncommonly still. Melissa marveled at Violet's power. "That's my best friend," she thought proudly. Violet waited a beat, then she began.

"My name is Violet Sparks," she said, "and I have an older brother who calls me George. What did I do to deserve this?" She paused. "I was born."

"He swatted a disgusting, gross, hairy fly on my head in public. And what did I do to deserve that? I was born.

"He did hundreds of other things too. Hundreds of them. Like he put lizards in my bed, fed me dog biscuits, wrote in my diary."

"Did he read the diary too?" yelled a younger.

"What do you think?" Violet waved a thick, rolled-up piece of paper. "Here, get a load of this." She unrolled and unrolled and unrolled until the paper, which was actually ten sheets Scotch-taped together, was as tall as she. "This is a complete list of his horrible tortures."

While kids craned their necks to view the enormous sheet of paper covered with Violet's handwriting in royal blue marker, she charged on.

"Every kid in this room has one thing we share. We may be good at math or spelling. We may play video games or soccer. Whatever," said Violet. "But in each of our homes lives an older brother or sister who resents us. Every single one of us could fill up a page this long with what our older brother or sister did to us. And what did we ever do to them?" Violet wasn't just asking, she was commanding. "We were just—," she thrust her fist in the air, and everyone shouted, "Born!"

Before Melissa knew what she was doing, her fist was in the air, too, and she was standing up. Everyone was.

"Maybe it all started a million years ago in some age like Mesozoic," Violet continued. "Maybe one day a chimpanzee refused to share a banana with his younger sister and then ate the whole thing right in front of her. Maybe that's when it started. But the question is, when will it stop? I say the time is now!"

Everyone cheered and stomped. Davy waved his fire helmet. Mugs barked, Ivy meowed, and Alfred said, "I'm Alfred, I'm Alfred, I'm Alfred."

Violet's voice boomed out: "Why do they hate us?"

Everyone shouted, "Because we were born."

"When will it stop?"

"Now."

"When will it stop?"

"Now!"

"When will it stop?"

"Nowwwwwwwwww!"

Cynthia was pulling on Melissa's sleeve. Melissa shook her arm free as Violet shouted, "Everyone repeat after me: Older brothers and sisters are vomitrocious."

Melissa yelled with the group, "Older brothers and sisters are vomitrocious." Cynthia tugged again.

"Cynthia, cut it out."

"But look." She pointed at the stage.

The curtain moved behind Violet. Not a lot. In fact, Melissa wasn't sure it had, but then it moved again. Melissa screamed, "A spy, a spy, a spy!"

Violet looked behind her with confusion as Melissa and Cynthia vaulted onto the stage. Melissa got there first and threw herself at the curtain. She could barely get her arms around it. She heard sounds—well, little squeaks mostly—but then Cynthia landed on top of her, and, as they wrestled the blob to the ground, the struggling stopped and the squeaking, too.

The kids were all out of their seats, crowding the stage. "Spy, spy, spy," they chanted.

Violet raised her arms high for everyone to calm down. Instantly there was silence. She moved through the crowd. "Release the prisoner," she ordered. Melissa and Cynthia let go and snapped to attention. "Good grief, it works. This general stuff works," thought Violet. She stood over the blob in her best I-am-tough position—legs apart, arms akimbo with her fists jabbed into her hips. The blob didn't move. "Uh-oh, Number 9," said Cynthia. "Death by Curtain Suffocation."

"Not quite." Violet pulled the curtain off.

Annabel DeMot lay on the floor, curled up like a puppy waiting for someone to rub its tummy. "Hi, Violet," said Annabel. "I want to join."

"Don't let her, she could be a spy," cried Melissa. "Maybe the olders paid her to come here. She's got no reason to be loyal to anyone. She's an"—Melissa hissed the words—"only child."

"It's not my fault," wailed Annabel.

"Kick her out," shouted someone.

"Yeah," yelled another. "Kick out the only."

Everyone started chanting, "Kick out the only, kick out the only."

Annabel was crying, "I don't want to go."

Violet waited until the chanting died down. "Never act rashly," she announced, realizing that this was her fourth rule of war, and a lot like her third, "Keep calm no matter what." She hoped she would remember it so she could write it down later. Maybe she needed a secretary.

"Take your seats," said Violet. "We're going to discuss our first prisoner."

"I'm a prisoner?" asked Annabel. "A pretend prisoner, right?"

Violet paced up and down the stage. Annabel sat on the floor, nervously chewing on her lower lip.

"Hey, try Number 17," said Cynthia.

"What's that?" asked Violet.

"Death by Ignoring. Here, I'll read it." Cynthia opened her book. " 'Nobody would speak to her. She'd say hello. No answer. She'd say, "Can I play?" People would look past as if she were invisible. Finally after fifteen years, she shriveled up and withered away.' "

"Fifteen years is too long to wait," said Violet.

"There are shorter deaths," said Cynthia.

"We should save them for the enemy. Just kidding," added Violet, noticing that Melissa's face had gone white at the thought. "If we turn Annabel loose, she might betray us."

"I wouldn't. I really wouldn't."

"The prisoner is not allowed to speak."

"My lips are sealed." Annabel pretended to zipper her mouth the way her mom had showed her.

Violet took a deep breath, and reminded herself that even George Washington and Napoleon must have had prisoners as idiotic as Annabel.

"We have to let her join," said Violet.

Annabel threw her arms around Violet. "I'll be good, I'll be so good."

"Didn't I tell you? No hugging."

"Aye, aye, General." Annabel gave her Brownie salute.

"Raise your right hand." Annabel did.

"Repeat after me: 'I swear to be loyal to the youngers and not to rest until they are avenged. I will fight the olders 'til I drop.'"

"I swear to everything," said Annabel. "You know what?"

"What?"

"Now I'm the only younger sister in the whole world who is an only child. I'm unique."

"Sit down and shut up," said Violet. Then she disappeared backstage and turned out the lights.

"Is there going to be a movie?" Melissa wondered as Violet flipped another switch. "Artie!" Melissa gasped.

Lit by a single spotlight, he stood in the center of the stage, alone. He was dressed 100 percent in purple—purple shoes, purple pants, and a purple shirt with silver stars decorating the collar. His black hair, normally combed straight back, was flipped forward into a single curl, which flopped around his nose. "Whoa, radical, check out the curl," said Cynthia.

Slung over his shoulder was a purple electric guitar.

"Introducing the great Artie Box," said Violet. Everyone clapped.

Artie strummed a bit and tapped his foot as if to signal, "Hold on, here we go." There was a second of silence, then boom, he hit the first chords. The amplified sound rocketed into the room. Artie started singing:

> *Give us strength,*
> *And give us courage,*
> *'Cause we're about to change the world.*
> *We're going to fight the olders,*
> *We'll never give in.*
> *We're going to fight the olders, aaand*
> *We're going to win.*

"Win, win, win, win, win, win, win." Everyone in the room chanted as Artie sang on.

"Being born second doesn't mean that we're dumb jerks, dopey, or berserk.

"We're up to here with torture—," Artie pointed to his knees.

"We're up to here with pain—," Artie pointed to his waist.

"They're gonna stop blaming us, pinching us, hitting us, tricking us. The youngers are coming, the youngers are coming, the youngers are coming, and we won't stop 'til we're through.

"Did you hear us?" Artie shouted. "We're going to get you!"

Everyone sang together:

> *Give us strength,*
> *And give us courage,*
> *'Cause we're about to change the world.*
> *We're going to fight the olders,*
> *We'll never give in.*
> *We're going to fight the olders, aaand*
> *We're going to win.*

Now Artie was jumping and gyrating, and everyone in the audience was, too, as he hit the chorus one more time. Melissa stood on her chair and blasted out the tune. Cynthia boogied with the boy next to her. Only Violet stood apart. Every shout, every cheer, every wiggle meant she had succeeded: This was war.

Once, in one of her true stories, Violet had read about a knight who was especially brave and strong-hearted. "That's like me," she had thought. "If I believe in something enough, I bet I can make it happen." Now that she knew for sure, the responsibility was awesome. It wasn't her fault, of course—Simon's hideous, relentless, revolting behavior had made war inevitable. He'd driven her to it. Boy, was he going to be sorry. He was going to be sick with sorry. The thought made Violet feel great.

CHAPTER FIVE

In which Violet teaches trickiness, Davy teaches the wrong thing, and Claire Sparks hears the battle cry

When Violet woke up the day after her great rally, she knew exactly where her hideout and training camp should be. "I even figure things out in my dreams," she congratulated herself as she got dressed in record time. She sat down at her desk, and opened the three-ring notebook where all her war plans were kept. There was her famous sayings sheet. It had two sayings so far: The fly may have died, but the war has begun; and Olders are vomitrocious. There were General Violet Sparks's Rules of Combat: (1) Never let the enemy know what's coming, (2) Learn to tell better lies, (3) Keep calm no matter what.

She added the fourth, the one she'd thought of yesterday: Never act rashly.

In the pocket inside the front cover was her map of Mountain Terrace. Violet pulled it out, and in dark red, the darkest red pencil she had, she outlined a large area behind the community center, just over the top of the hill.

This land was wild. There were no houses or roads. It was all dirt and sagebrush and large prickly bushes. There were strange twisted trees with short stubby branches. Violet called them fighter trees, because they looked like they were tougher than any other kind of tree and that's why they survived there. The fighter trees could hide and shelter the youngers. Parents would never find them. Nobody would, because nobody ever went there.

"But it's so prickly here," said Melissa as she and six other youngers sat on the hard dirt in a semicircle, waiting for Violet to begin their basic training session. Violet had broken the army into six groups.

"Get used to it," said Violet.

"But don't we need mats?" asked Melissa. "Aren't we going to learn pouncing or tackling?"

"No way. This is an army of the mind." Violet had borrowed a wand from Melissa's magic set, and she waved it in the air, swish, swish, for emphasis. "We shall win with our wits."

"What are wits?" asked Annabel.

"Wits are brains," said Violet, hoping that Annabel had some. "Now what does every soldier need?"

No one had a clue.

"Clothes?" asked Melissa.

That made Artie giggle. "A naked army," he snorted.

Violet ignored him. "Good guess," she said to Melissa, "but that's not the answer. Self-respect and trickiness. This technique I have invented combines both. Who wants to start?"

Cynthia raised her hand.

"Okay, pretend that you're Melissa's sister Suzette, and be really mean to Melissa."

Cynthia stood there, tying her braids together under her chin and thinking. "Okey-dokey, here goes. You smell like a sick whale and you look like death on toast, just kidding."

"No 'just kidding.' " Violet bounded over to Cynthia, waving her wand.

"Hey, watch out," said Cynthia.

"Try again. Try again and make it worse."

Cynthia looked at Melissa. "Hey, hot-dog brain, your lower lip looks like a frankfurter."

Melissa's head jerked up in shock. She blinked fast to beat back the tears.

"Don't cry," ordered Violet. She poked her in the chest. Then, like a ringmaster in a circus, she jumped back to the front. "Does everyone here know why not?" She whipped the wand around in a circle. "Be-

cause," she shouted, "because crying thrills the olders. So what do we do instead?"

Dead silence, except for a sniffle from Melissa.

"We smile."

"Smile?" Melissa's voice wobbled.

"You can do it," said Violet.

Melissa forced the ends of her lips out. She looked
goofy, like she was smiling but didn't get the joke.

"Good try," said Violet. "Now what are you thinking?"

"That I'm ugly."

"Wrong," said Violet, scratching her neck with the
wand. "Instead, think of something really nasty to call
her."

"To her face?" Melissa was horrified.

"No. Just some nasty secret thought."

"Uh, how about jerk?" said Melissa.

"Not nasty enough," said Violet.

"Creepola?" A real smile was breaking through.

"Much better. Can anyone think of something
else? Something vile." Annabel jumped up.

"Wart-headed, zit-faced fruit fly with elephant's
breath."

"Very good."

"I get it, I get it for sure," said Annabel, sitting back
down and smoothing her skirt.

"Does everyone understand?" said Violet. "Their

fun is making us freak out. So how do we stick it to
them?" She poked the wand into the air.

"Don't freak out!" everyone shouted.

"I am the great matador, Hernando, here to fight
the devil bull, olé." Simon grabbed his napkin and
waved it in front of Violet as he sat down to dinner.
"Is that a girl or a big ugly bull? Hard to tell. Oops."
He knocked over his milk glass. "It's George's fault.
He did it, she did it, whatever that is did it." He
pointed at Violet as Claire Sparks came in from the
kitchen.

"What happened?" she asked Violet.

"Oh, nothing. I'll clean it up." Violet jumped up
to get paper towels. She was following the exact instructions she'd been giving her troops. "Until the war
starts," she had told them, "be a doormat."

Claire Sparks beamed at her two children. "It's
been so peaceful here lately," she said as she watched
Violet wipe up the milk. "Are you going to the dance
this weekend, Simon?"

"Dances are dumb," said Simon.

Especially if you can't dance, thought Violet, but
she didn't say anything.

"Me and Bobby are going to a movie instead,

and then hanging out at the I-Hop. Don't wait up."
He leaned back in his chair and put his feet up on
the table. "I'm going to stay out probably until three."

"Probably until ten," said Claire Sparks, smiling.
"And take your feet down."

Probably until never, thought Violet, because that
day, three days from now, is Y-Day.

Violet's war plans were getting more and more
complicated. All the youngers had now been through
basic training. They'd learned mimicking. They'd
learned Violet's favorite trick—torture by dessert. A
small group, the hunters she called them, had been
ordered to catch lizards, which were stored in Cynthia
Ruggles's bedroom. Cynthia kept them in padlocked
cages because the worst, most gruesome death she'd
ever read about was Number 6, Death by Lizards.
They ate your toes one at a time, then worked their
way up. Number 6 required special African lizards,
but—who knew?—maybe one had swum the Atlan-
tic, walked across the U.S., and ended up in Mountain
Terrace.

"What's Y-Day?" asked Annabel.

"That's the day the war starts," said Violet pa-
tiently. "The *Y* stands for youngers." She was leading
her troops in their last exercise, making them repeat
the word *duh* over and over. "This is a very important

weapon," said Violet. "I call it the when-in-doubt word."

"I don't get it," said Melissa.

"Me neither," said Artie.

"You will," said Violet.

No one except Violet knew what Davy was up to. Every day after school, he took the animals to the basement in Violet's house. Violet's mom was working and Simon was playing basketball, so in this safe and quiet place, with no people around to make him nervous, Davy trained the animals according to Violet's precise instructions.

ORDERS TO DAVY BROWN,
HEAD OF THE ANIMAL BRIGADE
1. Teach Mugs to howl when he hears the song "My Bonnie Lies Over the Ocean."
2. Teach Ivy to jump on people's heads.
3. Teach Alfred three new words: Just like Arturo.

This last was the most difficult. Over and over, Davy said, "Just like Arturo." And over and over, Alfred answered, "I'm Alfred, I'm Alfred, I'm Alfred."

Davy blamed himself. Every time Alfred said, "I'm Alfred," Davy said, "I'm a dodo."

When Violet came to check on his progress, she found him sitting on the floor, crying and hiccupping. Violet patted him on the back.

"It won't work," said Davy. "Every time I say, 'Just like Arturo' he says, 'I'm Alfred.' Don't you, Alfred?"

Alfred fastened his beady eyes on Davy.

"Don't you?"

"I'm a dodo," said Alfred.

"What?"

"Congratulations," said Violet. "You taught him something."

"But it's the wrong thing."

"Keep up the good work," said Violet, and she left.

Nine hours to Y-Day. Violet, in her pink pajamas, stood in front of the mirror in her bedroom, practicing looks—ones to fear, ones to respect. She wielded her wand like a sword, imagining that Simon was cowering before her. "Eat worms. Shine my shoes. Crawl, slave."

Even though she didn't know much about music, she suspected that war was like a symphony. First you had a few notes, kind of like skirmishes. No one knew what they would amount to, until suddenly they turned into a melody—the battles. The melody got bigger and bigger, until it made a gigantic sound that definitely included cymbals—the final encounter. Then it got calm again as the melody faded out. That, thought Violet, would be when the youngers got peace on their terms.

She walked over to the window seat and sat down. She drew her legs up and wrapped her arms around them. She thought about her dad, who was living in San Francisco now. Every week when he called and asked what she was up to, she said, "Nothing."

"That's all you say?" Melissa was amazed.

"If he's not here, I'm not telling him anything," Violet had said matter-of-factly.

But, as Violet sat there, she thought she would like to tell her dad about her big plans for tomorrow. "What's new?" he would ask. "Oh, nothing, I'm just going to war." Ha! Wouldn't that freak him out?

Maybe he'll read about me, thought Violet. Maybe he'll open his morning paper and find his daughter on the front page. Violet grinned.

She looked out the window, down the block, at all the pink stucco houses with pots of geraniums on the front walks. I'm looking at the battlefield, thought

Violet. A shiver shot through her body and she hugged her legs tighter. " 'Give us strength, and give us courage.' "

Across the street, Melissa, in bed, tossed from one side to the other. Could she go to war? War! What a scary word. Even with wits and no guns, could she really see it through? She curled up into a little ball. "Fall asleep, please, fall asleep," she begged herself. She started humming, " 'Cause we're about to change the world.' "

Two streets over, Cynthia Ruggles was brushing her teeth. She could hear the lizards scampering in their cages. How would she ever get to sleep with them around?

She jumped into bed, and pulled the covers up so just her eyes peeked out. Suppose those lizards were chewing through the cages? Suppose they were going to crawl in bed with her any second? She pulled the covers all the way up, over her head. " 'The youngers are coming, the youngers are coming, the youngers are coming . . . ' "

Claire Sparks was out in the back yard. She'd been so busy working she hadn't had time to check her tomato plants. She was down on her knees with a flashlight, looking for bugs, when she heard something strange. That couldn't be crickets singing—the sound was so much sweeter.

She sat back on her heels and listened. She had no idea she was hearing the first sounds of war—a kind of battle cry—as younger brothers and sisters all over Mountain Terrace lay in bed, humming the fight song to give them peace for tonight and nerve for tomorrow.

CHAPTER SIX

In which the war sneaks up and clobbers the olders, and Annabel gets an aunt by accident

The youngers' alarm clocks all went off at 7:30 A.M. The clocks were like a single horn blowing reveille all over Mountain Terrace.

Violet had her clothes laid out. Lately she'd been wearing only black and white—black jeans and a white T-shirt. It was her uniform. She wore it for the sake of her troops, so they could always recognize her at least one block away.

Melissa felt like she hadn't slept at all; her head was buzzing with all Violet had taught her. Smile when they're mean; mimic; duh; keep calm no matter what. She looked in the mirror. She didn't look like a soldier and she didn't feel like one. She felt, well, limp. Like my hair, she thought.

Violet left her mom a note, saying she'd be spending the day with Melissa, and snuck out. She knew her mom wouldn't have time to check on her because she'd wake up late and have to rush out. Saturday was the busiest day at the store and her mom was expected at nine-thirty sharp. Above all, Violet didn't want to see Simon. He was the worst older, and late that night, he would be getting the worst torture of all. Until then, she didn't want to have anything to do with him. In the meantime, she had big responsibilities. Her troops needed her.

Violet headed for the community center. She passed Melissa's dad, who was out jogging, and she waved as if this might be any Saturday morning, and not the Beginning, with a capital *B*, of the end.

The center was deserted except for an early-bird workout. As she slipped quickly past the door to the gym, Violet saw Cynthia's mom pedaling an exercycle. If I live to a hundred, thought Violet, I never want to pedal a bike that goes nowhere. She stopped at the bulletin board. She carefully tacked up a notice. In large capital letters it said, OUR TIME HAS COME.

The announcement was scary, but vague. Violet wanted the war to sneak up on the olders and clobber them.

Melissa forced herself down the hall to the kitchen. She heard Suzette yakking about the dance.

"Guess what, Mom, I've named the food after hairdos, would you believe? Pageboy punch, crew cut pizza."

"Maybe we should name the baby after a hairdo, like Butch."

"That's no name for a girl," Melissa's dad shouted through the window. He'd finished jogging and was doing cool-down exercises.

"I wasn't serious," said Melissa's mom, slamming the window shut. "Eat your breakfast, Suzette."

Suzette stood there dreamily, a box of cornflakes in her hand. "Tonight I shall probably be queen of the dance. What smells weird? Oh," she acted as if she were totally shocked to see Melissa and gave a fake little jump. "P.U., it's you."

Melissa's eyes started to tear, but she caught herself. "Good morning," she said calmly while she frantically thought, Okay, think of a really awful name. Think! *Curly-headed codfish* popped into her brain and suddenly she didn't feel bad, just like Violet had said. Suddenly she was smiling.

"I said you smell."

"I do?" Melissa lifted her arm and sniffed. "Mmm, you're right, delicious." She offered a whiff to Max who had just walked in.

"I don't smell anything," said Max.

"Send this nutgirl to the nuthouse," said Suzette, tossing her hair forward and—

"Good idea," said Melissa, imagining that Violet was cheering her on.

"What did you say?" Suzette stopped mid-toss.

"What did you say?" said Melissa in exactly the same tone of voice.

"Melissa!" said Suzette.

"Melissa!" said Melissa.

"Make her stop," screamed Suzette.

"Make her stop," screamed Melissa.

"Sto-o-o-op!"

"Sto-o-o-op!"

"Melissa, would you stop it?" said Mrs. McFree.

"What makes you think it's Melissa's fault?" said Mr. McFree, walking in the back door.

Melissa's mom put her hand on her hip and cocked her head to one side. "Why aren't you ever on my side?"

"Why aren't you ever on mine?"

"I am."

"No, you're not."

Melissa backed out of the room while her parents were arguing, then grabbed the phone and dialed. The machine answered at Violet's. Melissa waited for the beep. "Message for Violet from me, Melissa. It's working!"

"What's working?" asked Max.

Fortunately, at that moment the telephone rang.

Melissa answered it. "I'm sorry she's not here," said Melissa and hung up.

"Was that for me?" Suzette shot into the hall.

"Yes."

"Who was it?"

"I forgot to ask."

"Male or female?"

Melissa pretended to think. "Which?" screamed Suzette.

"I think it was . . . male."

"And you didn't ask? You didn't ask?" Suzette's face was practically purple.

The phone rang again. Suzette grabbed it. "It's for you." She handed the phone to Melissa.

"Listen to this," said Cynthia before Melissa could say hi. "I saved my chocolate cake from last night. So while he's eating boring Cheerios, I eat it right in front of him. He goes, 'Can I have some?' I go, 'No.' I wag my chocolate tongue in his face. I'm gonna wag it again!"

"Hip, hip, hooray!" shouted Cynthia. "Torture by dessert." Melissa heard Bobby shriek, "Sto-o-o-op!"

Violet stood at the top of the hill, listening to the wails, shrieks, and screams of olders, listening to doors slam and feet stamp. "The first shots have been fired and the enemy's already wounded. Yes!" She puffed up her chest and stood tall. "This way!" she waved, as youngers tore out of their homes and raced up the hill to the hideout.

"Calm down, cool out." Violet had to shout to be heard as she led her excited troops through the sagebrush, trees and prickly bushes. She stopped where several fighter trees formed an especially hidden and private place.

"Attention," she cried, but still the youngers couldn't stop talking, slapping palms, and demonstrating how the various olders had gone berserk that morning.

Violet took her wand and banged it against the board, where she had tacked up her map and a special battle plan, written in forest green to match the trees. She banged it again. After a few more happy palm slaps, the youngers got quiet.

"Great job," she said. Everyone starting screaming and cheering all over again. She banged the wand.

"Private Ruggles will be handing out shovels to those soldiers on trap-digging detail— " She stopped. She noticed Artie. He was plopped on the ground, his head drooping over his shoes. "What's wrong?"

"Gabriel liked it," he moaned. "I mimicked him, and he liked it."

"So you're feeling sorry for yourself?"

"No," said Artie. "Yes." He moaned again. "Gabriel said, 'Arturo' "—Artie imitated Gabriel's snotty voice—" 'Arturo, do you want me to speak slowly, so you can get every word exactly?' and then, listen to this! Then my mom said, 'My sweet cannoli, soon you'll be speaking *just like Gabriel* on your own without having to repeat him.' " Artie rocked his head in his hands.

Cynthia handed him a shovel. "Don't burst a blood vessel."

"Good advice," said Violet. "Besides, you'll get another chance to get him. Attention!"

Artie jumped up, snapped his heels together and pulled his shoulders back. "Doesn't that make you feel better?" Violet asked.

He nodded.

"Now start digging."

"What's this trap for anyway?" Artie asked as he tossed his first shovelful of dirt over his shoulder.

Violet permitted herself a smile. "We're going to scare Simon like he's never been scared before."

There was awed silence.

Annabel DeMot pulled her little red wagon to the entrance to the community center parking lot. This is the perfect place, she decided. This is where I used to sell lemonade when I was practically a baby.

She opened a paper bag and took out one of her mother's bowls. Into it she squirted two cans' worth of shaving cream. She placed the bowl in the center of the wagon, and balanced a sign on the handle. The sign said, ANNABEL'S ICE CREAM. FREE.

Margaret Brown was bicycling to her ballet class when she saw Annabel and the little red wagon.

"I could see your sign a whole block away," she said. "I have perfect vision, which is almost as rare as perfect pitch. That doesn't look like ice cream."

"It's special super-duper soft ice cream," said Annabel.

"I can name every ice cream flavor in the world, and my dodo brother Davy can name only one, strawberry."

Annabel put a scoop on a cone and handed it to Margaret. "Have some. It makes your brain bigger."

"Mine's enormous already, but thank you." She took the cone. "When I lick, you might want to catch a glimpse of my perfect pink tongue."

"I'm watching," said Annabel.

Margaret licked. "Mmmmmm, de—" She was probably going to say *delicious*, but the next sound out of her mouth was gruesome, hideous, grotesque. She dropped the cone; she dropped the bike. She spit, she retched. Annabel had a glass of water handy. "Here, dearie," she said, trying to sound like a wicked witch. Margaret grabbed it and drank. The shaving cream foamed up, and her mouth turned into a bubble dispenser.

"You beast, you nasty beast." With each word, a large bubble popped out of Margaret's mouth and floated away.

Annabel crowed, "You think you can name all the ice creams. Well, I bet you didn't know Shaving Cream Swirl."

Annabel grabbed the wagon by the handle and ran. Her mind was spinning as fast as the wagon's wheels. I'll set myself up on the mini-mall, she thought. I can knock off twenty-five olders an hour. Maybe I'll put rocks in the shaving cream and call it Rocky Road. "Annabel's Ice Cream," she shouted. "Come and get it."

By three o'clock, her fifteenth older had fallen to his knees groaning. Annabel whipped her finger through what was left of the vanilla and drew a white mustache on the older's face before racing off. She was in the supermarket parking lot behind the mini-mall when Violet and Melissa walked up.

"Violet, guess what? I got Margaret, then I got fourteen other olders, Cynthia's Aunt Esther—"

"You got an aunt? This isn't a war against aunts."

"But it was an accident."

"Attention," said Violet in her best military voice. "And don't speak."

"Okay, oh boy," said Annabel, zippering her mouth.

This calls for judgment, thought Violet. This may be my first big moment of judgment. "You injured a regular person who is not an older. For this there are consequences."

"Conse-whats?"

"You do something bad, you get in trouble," barked Violet. "Get it?"

"Uh-oh," said Annabel.

"You are sentenced to one hour's solitary confinement. Just go off by yourself."

Annabel started wailing. "But I don't want to, I can't, it's not fair— " She stopped. She got a funny look on her face.

Violet got a worrisome feeling that that look meant that Annabel was actually thinking. Was this possible, and was it good?

"You're right, General," said Annabel. "I should be punished. I'll spend my time alone thinking of new ways to get the creeps." She saluted and made a smart, sharp turn. As she marched off, Violet and Melissa heard her say, "Ooh, neat, solitary."

Melissa put her hand on Violet's arm. "She's just a baby."

"I don't know what you're talking about," snapped Violet. She put her hands behind her back and clasped them. It seemed to her that in some book somewhere she'd seen a picture of a general talking to his troops with his hands clasped in exactly that way.

"What ho, General," said Cynthia, breezing up on her bike. In her basket, rattling against one another, were several mayonnaise jars, each with holes punched in the top and a lizard inside. "Here are your juicy reptiles."

"Thank you," said Violet.

"Why are you wearing gloves?" asked Melissa.

"To avoid Number 28, Death by Tropical Disease, natch," said Cynthia.

"Violet, I don't get it," said Melissa. "How come we're using lizards on the olders when Simon already used them on you? Isn't that copying?"

"Of course it's copying. That's the whole point. So they find out what it feels like."

"Oh." Melissa grinned. "That's so smart."

"You bet." Violet handed Melissa a large yellow envelope. "This is for you, and for you only. Instructions are inside. Read and destroy."

CHAPTER SEVEN

In which Violet tells half the truth, and Suzette's hair hits and sticks

Violet opened her basement door and peered down. In the glow of the single light bulb hanging from the ceiling, she could see Davy. He was giving Ivy the thumbs-up sign. Ivy jumped from a ceiling pipe onto his head.

"Good job," said Davy. He petted Ivy and gave her some catnip.

"Great," said Violet, coming down the stairs.

"Okay, ready?" he asked Mugs, who was lying on a towel having a nap. Mugs sat up.

"My Bonnie lies over the ocean," sang Davy. His voice was as squeaky as nails on a blackboard. Mugs howled; he rolled over. Davy gave Mugs a dog biscuit and scratched him behind his ears. "Okay, Alfred, your turn. What do you say?"

"I'm a dodo," said Alfred.

"Still, still, still!" Davy smashed his hand into his forehead.

"Violet? Violet, are you there?" Claire Sparks peeked in. "Oh, hi, Davy."

"Uh, hi," said Davy.

"Do I see a dog down there?" Claire Sparks took off her sunglasses and stuck her neck way inside the door. "Good grief, there's an entire zoo. Do the owners of these animals know they're here?"

Davy's voice quaked. "I asked per—, per—"

"Permission," said Violet. "He asked permission."

"Oh, that's a relief. But what are they doing here?"

"What they're doing here is—," Violet started thinking frantically, Tell better lies, tell better lies. "Davy's training animals."

"I'm a dodo," said Alfred.

"You taught him that? How clever," said Mrs. Sparks. "Well, have fun." She closed the door.

"That's amazing," said Violet. "I thought I should tell a lie. I even had a rule about it. But I just found out it's better to tell half the truth." Violet let herself smile. It was a big, happy, relaxed smile.

"You know what, Violet?"

"What?"

"I wish I could live my whole life in this basement and never see my sister again."

"You have to face your fear," Violet said. "In fact,

I've brought you something to help you do it." She handed him a mayonnaise jar with a very fat lizard inside.

"Do I have to? Please don't make me."

Violet put her arm around him. "You'll make yourself."

Melissa sat on her bed and slit open the large manila envelope marked TOP SECRET. As she read, she started giggling. She giggled harder. She couldn't stop. She mashed her face into her pillow so no one could hear. Suzette was going to beg for mercy. Beg for it! Melissa suddenly sat straight up. Could she do it?

She tore the battle plan into tiny pieces and flushed them down the toilet. She was following Violet's instructions exactly. Then she opened the second envelope and removed a piece of flypaper. She held it gingerly, by the edges.

"What's that?" asked Max, walking in.

"Nothing," said Melissa.

He reached out to touch it. "Don't," said Melissa. "It's sticky. If flies touch it, they get glued on forever."

"Would you do that to a fly?" Max asked.

"Never. But I'd do it to a spider," Melissa said,

thinking of Suzette. "Don't tell anyone I have it, okay?"

"Is it for the war?"

"Yes."

"I love you, Melissa."

"I love you, too, Maxy-doodle. You know the difference between me and Suzette? One of the biggest big differences? Her nicknames are mean and cruel, and mine are totally loving. Wish me luck."

"Can I come?"

"Yes, but don't say anything."

Hiding the flypaper behind her back, Melissa walked down the hall to the kitchen. Max followed. They could hear Suzette.

"Oh, don't touch my nails, the polish is drying. Mom, I'm never going to be ready, never—just doing my hair is going to take hours. How do you like my eyelashes, I've sprinkled on glitter?" She batted her eyes.

Max and Melissa walked in. "Hi, Suzette," said Max.

"Squelch it, shrimp."

The doorbell rang. "It's probably my corsage," said Suzette, flouncing off. She opened the door. "Rats."

"Hi, Suzette," said Annabel DeMot. "Hi, Mrs. McFree. Hi, Melissa, hi, Max."

Oh, no, what was she doing here, now of all times? Melissa glared at her. Annabel winked.

Suzette flounced back into the kitchen. "Well, I guess I'll go dress for the dance."

"Wait," said Melissa.

"Ugh, why are you so close? I don't want your cooties, what is it?"

Melissa's mind went suddenly blank.

Annabel chirped up, "Can I take your picture? You're so pretty." She held up a small camera.

"Of course," said Suzette. She put a hand on her hip and tilted her chin up. "I'm not going to smile, so don't ask me. It's too immature."

As Annabel pretended to focus, she gave the tiniest jerk of her shoulder toward Suzette. Melissa knew instantly what she was supposed to do. She moved very close to her sister. "What about your hair, Suzette?" asked Melissa sweetly. "Don't you want to toss it?"

Suzette flipped her head down, and, as she tossed her hair forward, Melissa whipped out the flypaper. Boing, Suzette's hair hit and stuck. "Eu, eu, eu," screamed Suzette.

"What happened?" asked Mrs. McFree, who had been looking in the refrigerator for eggs.

"Oh, an accident, a terrible accident," cried Annabel, pretending to pull the flypaper out but actually mushing it in more.

"Yes, an accident," Melissa said faintly.

"It wasn't, it wasn't!" shrieked Suzette.

"What was the flypaper for, anyway?" asked Mrs. McFree.

"For?" Melissa didn't know what to say. Violet hadn't put anything about that in the plans. She hadn't said Melissa would have to lie to her mother, either. "It was for . . . "

"Flies," said Annabel. "We're catching them." Melissa kept silent.

Mrs. McFree examined Suzette's head. "I'm afraid we're going to have to cut your hair."

"I'll be practically bald," cried Suzette.

"There's no point in crying. It'll grow back. In the meantime, you'll have to go to the dance as a famous person with short hair. With very short hair," she added, looking more closely at the damage done by the flypaper. "Now who could you be?"

"Humpty Dumpty?" said Max.

"Tweedledum or Tweedledee?" said Melissa.

Suzette wailed. Melissa scrunched her lips together so she wouldn't laugh. Annabel giggled. So did Max. "I hate you. I hate all of you!" screamed Suzette.

"There, there," said Mrs. McFree. "I have the perfect solution. We'll put a turban on your head. You'll go as Olga, a famous Turkish dancer."

"How famous was she?" Suzette sniffled.

Mrs. McFree took a pair of scissors out of the kitchen drawer. "Very," she said.

CHAPTER EIGHT

In which Violet gets a bad kiss, and Davy gets a good one

Right after dinner, Violet knocked on Melissa's bedroom window.

"Hold it, one second," said Melissa. She ran back behind the doorway where she and Max had been hiding, watching Jock pick up Suzette for the dance. Jock was barefoot, and wearing cut-off jeans and a T-shirt with a peace sign on it. His hair, a mop he'd removed from the handle, came down to his shoulders. Melissa heard him say, "Peace and love, here's your hippie, babe. Don't look now, but there's a mountain on your head."

"It's called a turban." Suzette gently patted the blue scarf that her mom had wrapped tightly around her head and secured with a silver pin at center front. "I hope none of my hair is showing."

"She hardly has any," Melissa whispered, giggling. Then she climbed out the window and joined Violet, Davy, and the animals.

"Step one, my place," said Violet. They ran across the street.

Violet entered first and checked Simon's bedroom. She gave the all-clear sign. They opened the closet and put Mugs inside. "I'm counting on you," said Davy, giving Mugs several dog biscuits. He covered him with a blanket.

"Well, if it isn't fat George," said Simon.

Violet slammed the door, closing in Mugs and Davy with Alfred on his head.

"What are you doing in my room?" Simon stood in the doorway. He wasn't wearing a shirt, and his hair was sopping wet from trying to get his cowlick to lie down.

"We thought you left and we were playing hide-and-seek—" Hide-and-seek? Violet couldn't believe she'd said that. It was a kids' game, she hadn't played it since she was eight. "Davy came in by accident." Violet opened the closet really fast, pulled Davy out, and slammed the door shut again.

Simon looked down at Davy, then raised his eyes slightly to Alfred. "Don't look now, but there's a chicken on your head."

Violet laughed as if that were the funniest thing in the world.

"You think that's funny, huh?" Simon started circling Violet, Melissa, and Davy. "There's something fishy going on here."

Violet held her breath—don't look in the closet. Simon whipped open the closet door. Not a sound. The blanket with Mugs under it made a little lump on the floor. It was barely visible next to all the old sneakers, soccer balls, and dirty socks and underwear.

The doorbell rang.

"That's for you, Simon sweetie." Mrs. Sparks poked her head in. "Give me a kiss."

Simon pulled on his T-shirt and kissed his mom. "Why don't you kiss Violet too?" she said. "You never kiss your sister."

Simon held his nose.

"Come on," said Claire Sparks. "For me."

"This isn't happening, this isn't happening, this isn't happening," thought Violet as Simon walked toward her with a smirk on his face. "Give me strength, and give me courage." Violet closed her eyes as she felt his horrible skinny lips brush her cheek.

Melissa looked straight at the ground. She would rather die than look at Violet right now.

"Oh, that was so nice." Mrs. Sparks went back down the hall. "Don't stay too late at the I-Hop, Simon."

The doorbell rang again.

"This is good-bye for now," whispered Simon. He shook his head. All the water flew off his wet hair. Melissa squealed, Alfred squawked. Violet managed not to say anything, although she was soaked.

As soon as she heard the front door slam, she ran into the bathroom and started scrubbing her cheek hard with a washcloth and soap.

"That was the worst," said Melissa. "I can't believe you're related to him."

"I won't be for long," said Violet, hanging up the washcloth. "Let's hit Artie's."

"Good news," said Artie, opening the front door. "My parents are at a Mozart concert and Gabriel is at the dance selling ponytail pop. We don't even need to hurry. I hope this works."

"Me, too," said Davy.

"It will," said Violet.

"But nothing has," said Artie. "I'm a flop."

"Don't say that," said Violet.

They went down the hall to Gabriel's bedroom. The walls were covered with blue ribbons that he had won at violin recitals. "It must be hard to have a brother who has so many awards," said Melissa.

"Is it ever!"

They put Alfred in Gabriel's closet. Before they closed the door, Davy said, "Just like Arturo," one last time. Alfred didn't respond.

"At least he didn't say, 'I'm a dodo.' Isn't that a good sign?" said Davy.

"Yes," said Violet.

"I hope so." Davy looked wistfully at Alfred.

Alfred nipped Davy's cheek.

"He kissed you," said Melissa.

"Oh, no." Davy slapped his hand to his cheek. "That's what Simon did to Violet."

"It's not the same," said Violet. "Not in a million years."

CHAPTER NINE

In which hippie meets baldy, and Annabel pops her cork

Holding up branches to hide themselves, Violet, Melissa, and Davy moved along with the crowd. No one going to the dance noticed that the trees along the path were moving with them. They were too busy talking.

"Did you hear about Sammy? Some twerp fed him shaving cream."

"Spencer finked out on Sara. His little brother gave him the flu. On purpose."

"She repeated everything I said. I was screaming."

"Same here."

"Whose time has come?"

Melissa poked Violet. "It's working. Boy, is it ever working."

They couldn't help staring at the hairdos. One girl came as Little Bo Peep, with yellow ringlets and curls.

"Ooh, Elvis," said Melissa, peering through her branch at a boy who had greased-up black hair and kept swinging his hips when he walked. Rapunzel's hair was there, too—a girl with a huge skein of yellow yarn dropping from her head to the floor.

"Okay, ditch your branches and stick close, nobody will notice us," said Violet.

To Melissa's amazement, Violet was right. Everyone was so busy admiring one another's hair that no one saw three kids and a cat scoot into the gym.

The first thing Violet noticed were the signs posted all around: HAIR SPRAY HOT DOGS, PERMANENT POTATO CHIPS, PONYTAIL POP. She ducked behind a booth that said, FRENCH FRIES—CURLY OR STRAIGHT. Here they were hidden but had a terrific view.

Hanging from the ceiling were crepe paper streamers with big pink rollers tied to the ends. Bobbing between these were helium balloons. "Look at that, they've got wigs on them," said Melissa, amazed. "How strange," said Violet, staring at the blond, brunette and redheaded balloons, balloons with bangs, balloons with braids, and even one with a flat-top. Suzette had drawn faces on the balloons and they looked like bodiless heads floating in space.

"I don't like them," said Davy.

Suzette twirled around on the dance floor underneath her creations, accepting compliments on them with a fake little smile. Every so often she licked her lips because she had read in a magazine that boys prefer moist lips to dry ones.

"I could drown in your eyes," said Jock. "I could swim in your cheeks."

"Oh, Jock," sighed Suzette.

"You won't be smiling soon," thought Melissa.

"You bet," said Violet, reading her thoughts.

A band called the Bobby Pins was playing rock 'n' roll. Hanging from wires directly above the bandstand were a brush and comb big enough to coif a giant.

Violet stared. "We have to get Ivy up there."

"She can do it," said Davy.

He cradled Ivy in his arms. He stroked her on the head and scratched behind her ears. He talked to her softly. Then he put her down.

Ivy moved quickly, scooting along the back of the booth. From there she jumped onto one of the hair rollers suspended by a streamer, and before her weight could break it off, she jumped to another, then another and another.

"May I have your attention?" Jock spoke into the microphone on the bandstand. "Welcome to the Hair Ball." Everyone clapped.

A fat lock of his mop fell into his face, and he

brushed it back. "Ugh, this mop smells," he said, "but that's not why I'm here. I'm going to crown the queen." He waved a sealed envelope in the air. "The queen of the ball has been chosen by popular vote, and the winner is," he opened the envelope, "Suzette McFree."

"Eeek," Suzette squealed. "It's me, I can't believe it's me."

"Where's Ivy?" asked Melissa.

"She's almost there," said Violet, whose eyes were glued to the flash of black lightning as Ivy bounced from roller to roller.

Giggling and eeeking, Suzette made her way through the crowd to the bandstand. She twirled once so that everyone could see her dress. "Like my sarong?" she said. "My mom made it out of a bed sheet." Then she clasped her hands in front of her heart so that she would look sincere. "I would like to thank everyone for making me queen. This honor makes me feel so humble and—"

"Conceited," someone shouted.

"Huh? Who said that?"

Silence.

"Well, as I was saying, this honor makes me feel humble and—"

"Sickening," came the voice again.

"That sounds like Annabel," said Davy.

"You're right, it does," said Melissa. "She's not supposed to be here, is she?"

"It's not in her battle plan," said Violet.

"Whoever's saying those mean things, shut up, just shut up," said Suzette. "Now back to what I was saying. What was I saying?"

Before she could figure it out, Ivy reached the gigantic brush directly above Suzette's head. Davy gave the thumbs-up sign, and . . .

Ivy jumped. She landed on Suzette's head. Her claws sank into the turban. "Eu, get it off, get it off," screamed Suzette, shaking her head. Ivy dug in her claws as if each of her nine lives depended on it. "Jock, help!"

Jock grabbed Ivy and pulled. The turban came off with her.

"Aaaaaaaaaaa!" Suzette shrieked. She covered her head with her hands.

"What happened to your hair?" demanded Jock. "Good grief, I'm out with a baldy."

"My hair's just short," screamed Suzette. "All you ever think about's yourself."

"Look who's talking."

"Hippie, huppie, baldy," screamed a voice.

"Oh my gosh, it's Annabel again." Melissa

couldn't believe what was happening to her sister in public.

Everyone was trying to get a look at her. Some kids were laughing. Some thought it was mean to laugh but couldn't help it. One boy was so convulsed, he was rolling around on the floor.

"I'm humiliated," screamed Suzette. She ran through the crowd, dodging kids who tried to stop her. "Let me go," cried Suzette. She ran out the door.

The spotlight still shone on the bandstand. No one noticed that a little girl was there now. Her arms were raised to the sky, her hands wiggled and shook. "Hey, ho, Baldy's dead. Get the creeps, get the creeps, get the creeps." With that, she took the same path Suzette had taken and she tore out.

Violet watched Annabel streak through the crowd. "She's popped her cork," said Violet to no one in particular.

Annabel screeched to a stop at the community center bulletin board. She put a big X through the sign OUR TIME HAS COME and wrote above it in gigantic letters, OLDERS ARE VOMITROCIOUS. Then she let out a howl, a kind of war-crazed battle cry, and raced out into the night, leaping over hedges, cutting through flower beds. "Creeps, creeps, creeps," she chanted as she charged into her house.

"Where on earth have you been?" said her mom.

"Out."

"Just out?"

"I only answer to the general. Torture me, put me on the rack. I don't care."

"Annabel, what's the matter with you? Cynthia's aunt called. She said you fed her shaving cream and told her it was ice cream."

"I did!" Annabel jumped up on the couch, dashed across the cushions, leapt off the arm, and, pretending she had a machine gun in her hands, went, "E-e-e-e-e-e."

"I don't allow guns and I don't allow gunplay," said Mrs. DeMot. "Sit down right now."

Annabel snapped to attention, saluted, and sat on the couch.

"I have something wonderful to tell you."

"Oh yeah?" said Annabel.

"You're going to be an older sister."

"Huh?"

"I'm pregnant. I'm going to have a baby."

"Noooooooo!" Annabel screamed. "No, no, no, no, no." She put her hands over her ears.

"I thought you'd be happy."

"I won't be an older. I won't. They're horrible, they're disgusting, they're vomitrocious."

"Of course they're not."

Annabel yelled with her mouth so wide open you could practically see to China. "NOOOOOOOO!"

CHAPTER TEN

In which Simon sees crazy blue eyes, is tied up like a roast chicken, and lands on his funny bone

Simon pushed his coffee cup away. "That's a record," he said to Bobby. "Six cups."

Bobby ran his finger across his plate to get the last of the cherry sauce he'd poured on his pancakes, then followed Simon up to the cash register.

"Wasn't that cool in the movie when that guy just went zap, zap, zap?" said Bobby as they left the I-Hop.

Simon grabbed a stick and zigzagged a *Z* across Bobby's chest. "Zap, zap, zap. You can't catch me," shouted Simon. He ran across the street and up the hill to Ravencrest Drive.

Melissa trailed down the street after Violet. She'd barely noticed when they dropped off Davy. She

hadn't even heard Violet say, "Good luck with the lizard." Her mind was elsewhere, glorying in the night's
events. She felt powerful, dangerous, brilliant. Over
and over she replayed the evening, especially Suzette's snobby little speech and then the turban flying
off. Suzette had gotten hers in spades. Was she ever
going to think twice before picking on Melissa again.

"Goodnight," said Violet.

"Goodnight?"

"You're home," said Violet.

"I am? Oh, I am. Thanks."

Violet pointed to the front door just in case Melissa didn't see it. Melissa closed her eyes and savored
the moment. "What a wonderful feeling."

"It's victory," said Violet. "There's nothing like it.
See you later." Violet ran across the street and beat it
into the house just as Simon, waving good-bye to
Bobby, came up the block.

Violet waited. She listened at the door of her bedroom, waiting. She heard Simon come in the door.
She heard him tell their mom every tedious detail of
the movie. She was in no rush. She'd spent her life
with that monstrosity of a brother and a few more
minutes wouldn't make any difference. The lizard
was tucked in. Mugs was stashed and ready. Melissa
and a corps of specially selected youngers would be
outside soon, hiding in the back, awaiting her signal.

"En garde, zap, zap, zap." Violet stiffened as she heard Simon fence his way down the hall, using a fireplace poker for a sword. He lunged into his room, putting the final, deadly thrust into his imaginary enemy. He bowed and accepted a medal from an imaginary king, then raised his arms to quiet imaginary throngs. "My friends," he said.

At the word "my," there was a growl.

"Hey, Mom," called Simon. "I think there's something in my closet."

"Don't be silly, honey," called his mom. "It's just your imagination after that scary movie."

Simon continued to fence as he brushed his teeth, tried saying "en garde" while he gargled, and then fenced his way into bed. "Who needs lights? Only cowards." He flipped the poker under the light cord and pulled the plug right out of the wall. He tossed the poker into the corner, and got into bed.

Something tickled his foot. He scratched. The tickle squiggled up to his knee, then to his thigh. Then he felt the tickle on his arm. Was it one, was it two? A single lizard was lounging on his thigh but, in Simon's panic, he madly multiplied it. Was there something on his shoulder? "It's black widow spiders," he moaned, "a million of them."

Simon tore off his pajamas and started wildly

brushing off his body. Suddenly he stopped. There was nothing. Nothing at all.

He felt his way over to his bureau and put on another pair of pajamas. He put the bottoms on first, backward by mistake because he couldn't see. He buttoned up the top, felt his way back to bed, and pulled back the covers. Two electric-blue eyes stared at him. They were tiny and glowed like miniature headlights. Simon backed away.

The eyes moved across the mattress. Simon took another step, tripped over the poker, and landed on his behind. Now the blue lights were on the floor, staring up at him. Simon slid. He used his hands, pushing against the floor. "Uh-auk"—his head cracked against the wall. He was wedged into a corner while the two unblinking eyes advanced. Simon was drenched with sweat. His mouth trembled, and then, without realizing it, he started singing. Faintly and tinnily, but definitely singing.

This is what Simon had always done when he'd been a little boy and something frightened him. He thought no one knew, but he was wrong. Violet knew. And she knew what song he sang. "My Bonnie lies—" He didn't get any further because he heard howling as Mugs, in the closet, tried to sing along.

Simon bolted out of the room.

"What is it, dear?" said Claire Sparks, keeping one eye on the TV, on Ted Koppel, who she thought was the cutest newscaster.

"There's something in my closet."

His mom smiled. "A monster, maybe? Or a wolf? Remember how you teased Violet that time? That was so funny."

"Funny?" thought Violet, listening at the door. "Funny like a skunk."

"This is for real," said Simon, "And crazy blue eyes are after me."

Violet strolled into the living room as if she didn't know every single second of what was happening. "What crazy blue eyes?"

"Never mind," said Simon.

"I think your brother's having a heebie-jeebie attack," said Claire Sparks.

"Aw, I was just kidding." Simon swaggered out, back down the hall. At least he thought he swaggered. To Violet, he seemed to lurch, like a seasick cow.

She ran to the window and blinked the flashlight once. "One flash, let's go," Melissa whispered to the other youngers.

Violet dropped the flashlight and ran back down the hall. "Oh, Simon, you forgot to close your door. Do you want me to do it?"

"Uh, sure," Simon gulped. Violet knew he'd be too embarrassed to admit he wanted the door open and every light on. She pulled the door closed, and he was back in the dark. "My Bonnie . . . ," his voice quaked.

"Aeoooooouw." The howling started again. Simon threw himself on the bed and put his hands over his ears. "M-om-my"—it came out like a squeak as he was pulled off the bed by his legs and a blanket was thrown over his head.

"Hup, two, three, four, older brothers will be no more. Hup, three, four, five, chop them up and eat them alive." Violet marched alongside her soldiers. Eight of them carried Simon, who was rolled up in the blanket. "What a tub of lard," said Cynthia, huffing along. Melissa carried her tool kit just in case, and the rest of the youngers provided camouflage, surrounding them with a dense shield of branches as they made their way to the wild.

Here it was darker, almost pitch-black. The youngers whipped out their flashlights. Soon there were little circles of light bobbing along, marking the way to the hideout.

"Unwrap the filthy hound," hissed Violet.

They dropped Simon on the ground, grabbed the

edge of the blanket, and pulled. Simon spun around a few times and flipped out. He lay there, his eyes open. Violet waved her hand in front of them. He didn't blink.

"Don't worry, he's not dead . . . yet," Violet announced.

The youngers started giggling. Melissa leaned down and whispered in his ear, "A dinosaur's going to get you," then she slapped her hand over her mouth in a fit of giggles.

"Attention," said Violet.

Melissa clicked her heels together and made a very sharp salute.

"At ease," said Violet, "but no giggling."

"Right," said Melissa, pressing her lips together, trying not to imagine that Suzette's head, mistaken for a bowling ball, was rolling down an alley and knocking down some pins.

Violet stood there, about as relaxed as she thought proper—feet apart, hands clasped behind her back. She kept her eyes on Simon. Soon he blinked a few times, and the fuzzy spots in front of his eyes disappeared. "Violet? Violet, is that you?" It was the first time in years he hadn't called her George. He jumped up and threw his arms around her.

"Down, swine," said Violet.

"Huh?"

The soldiers pulled him off her. Cynthia quickly tied a scarf over his eyes.

"Hey, stop it, let me go, what's going on?" Simon kicked, and his arms whirled like windmills, but Cynthia grabbed one arm and Melissa the other, and soon he was trussed up like one of Melissa's mother's roast chickens, which were always crisscrossed with string to keep the wings and legs in place.

"This is war," Violet said, "and you are the prisoner."

"Oh, sure," said Simon. "Don't make me laugh."

"It's us against you—all the younger sisters and brothers against all the olders."

"What did I ever do to you?" said Simon.

"What?" Violet whipped out her gigantic list and unrolled it. Every other younger whipped out a list, too. Their lists all reached from their heads to their toes. "This is everything you ever did to me," said Violet, shaking her list, "and that's everything their olders did to them. Get it?" She didn't wait for an answer. "Our war started this morning, and by noon tomorrow, the world will know. I am the general."

"Little General Violet, how cute."

"Shut up," screamed Melissa, "or you'll get yours like Suzette."

"Yeah," shouted the youngers.

"Silence," said Violet.

Every mouth clamped shut. The place was eerily silent.

"You'll never get away with this," Simon shouted as the youngers dragged him off. "Hey, you're hurting me." The youngers yanked him over rocks and twigs, toward a big pile of leaves. When they reached the edge, they gave him a shove with a little spin on it. Simon rolled fast toward the center.

"Bye," Violet said softly as Simon rolled into the leaves, hit the middle and dropped into the pit beneath. He landed on his funny bone.

"Hellllllllp," Simon moaned.

"I'm holding a book in my hands, Simon," said Violet. "It's called *Sixty Gruesome Ways to Die*. We're going to read it to you, which may take all night, and then I'm going to select your death."

"Yeah," shouted all the youngers.

"If our demands aren't met, you are history."

"We're going to ransom you, Simon, but it's not money we're after," said Melissa.

Violet stood at the edge of the pit and peered down. "I'm going to change the world," she said.

CHAPTER ELEVEN

In which the lizards are lively

Davy stood at his sister's bedroom door, trying to remember everything Violet had told him when she dropped him off after the dance. "Be brave. Believe in yourself. Trust the lizard." He kept repeating this, over and over, but still his knees banged together like bumper cars. He knew Margaret's room was empty because he could hear her across the hall in the bathroom, singing in the shower. He pushed open the door.

Above Margaret's bed on a piece of poster paper she had written her name sixteen different ways. Circling the poster paper, framing it like art, were her report cards, kindergarten through seventh grade. She'd never gotten a grade lower than an A. "Don't pay any attention," said Davy to himself. "You can train animals and she can't." He reached into his shirt pocket and pulled out the lizard.

It was a lively one. Its tongue was shooting in and

out. Davy tiptoed over to the bed.

"What are you doing here, dodo bird?" asked Margaret. Davy popped the lizard in his mouth and whipped around.

Margaret walked in, sopping wet and wrapped in a towel. Her round, popping eyes blinked rapidly as she stared down at him. "Got our rooms mixed up? Can't remember where yours is?"

Davy kept his mouth clamped shut. He could feel the lizard's tail tickling his tongue. He started to edge his way out of the room. "Well, goodnight, dummy," said Margaret.

"Tell her you're not!"—Davy could hear Violet's voice in his brain. "Let her have it," Violet urged. I will, thought Davy. Right now! He opened his mouth to speak, and the lizard slid down his throat.

Davy made a strange sound, something between a wail and a moan. His eyes watered up so that Margaret seemed to swim in front of him. "I, I, I—"

"What are you trying to say? Spit it out," snapped Margaret, adjusting her towel.

"I, I, I'm a dodo!" said Davy. He threw himself on the floor and sobbed.

Artie wasn't taking any chances. He had gotten

two lizards from Cynthia, and they were big. One even slurped when its tongue shot in and out. Both were napping right now in Gabriel's bed while Artie hid behind the curtain and pressed his back against the wall, trying to make himself flatter than a fried egg so he wouldn't be noticed.

Without being able to see, Artie knew exactly what Gabriel would do before he went to sleep because he did the same thing every night. "Like clockwork," his mother bragged. First he did fifteen push-ups and ten jumping jacks. Gabriel was the only kid Artie knew who had nauseating goals like being physically fit. Then he said his prayers, "Please God, help me practice the violin so that I may tour Europe and give all my earnings to charity, help me convince Arturo to give up rock 'n' roll, and God bless Chopin, Schubert, Beethoven, Bach, and Mozart. Yours truly, Gabriel Box. Amen."

"Okay," Artie whispered, "now he's getting up off his knees, he's turning down the blanket, he's getting into bed, he's turning out the light. Now scream, Gabriel, scream."

Artie waited.

"Cootchy, cootchy, coo," said Gabriel.

"Huh?"

"Cootchy, cootchy—oh, please, Mother, come

here." Gabriel sang the words "come here," one high, one low, as if he were a musical doorbell.

Artie was so agitated he stuck his head out from behind the curtain. "Oh, hi," said Gabriel, as if it were perfectly normal for Artie to be hiding there. Artie was too insulted to speak. Gabriel wasn't even mad at him. And, worse, one of the horrible lizards that Artie could barely stand to touch was licking Gabriel's ear and Gabriel liked it.

"Oh, don't, you're tickling me," Gabriel squealed. He took the lizard off his shoulder and kissed it right on the mouth. "Look at this darling lizard," he said to his mother as she walked in. "Wait a second, there's another in my pajamas." Gabriel stood up on his bed and shook his leg. A lizard fell out, making slurping sounds. "I think I'll sleep with them for a week, and write it up next year for my science experiment."

"Brilliant," said Antonia Box. "Why don't you sleep with lizards, too, Artie, just like . . . "

"AAAAIIIIIIII!" Artie bellowed, he shrieked, he blared. His gigantic wail of despair propelled him like jet fuel out of Gabriel's room and into his own. He slammed the door, jumped into bed, and pulled the blankets over his head. "I'm a failure, total and complete. For the rest of my life I'm going to be listening to 'Just like Gabriel, just like Gabriel, just like Gabriel.' I'll have to give up rock 'n' roll. I'll probably have to marry my violin."

"Arturo? Arturo, my tangy tartufo, are you all right?"

Artie buried his head in his pillow so he couldn't hear his mother's voice. He lay there in the dark, flooding his pillow with tears until it was as squishy as a wet sponge. He would resign from the army tomorrow. He'd ask Violet for a dishonorable discharge.

CHAPTER TWELVE

In which Violet selects from sixty gruesome ways to die

All night the youngers sat around the pit, eating popcorn and chips, drinking sodas, and reading one gruesome death after another. The fighter trees surrounded them like bodyguards, but in the darkness they could imagine bats and owls, strange sounds, and secret lives. "This is better than a slumber party," said Cynthia.

They took turns reading aloud: Death by Quicksand, Death by the Bloodsucking Spotted Shark. After each death Violet waved her wand and pronounced judgment. "No," she declared. She hadn't yet found exactly the right end for her brother, but every so often she hesitated before saying no, so Simon would go nuts with anxiety.

"Stop blubbering," she said at one point. "As far as you're concerned, I'm deaf."

"We're up to Number 50," said Cynthia. "Only ten left."

"My turn," said Melissa, taking the book. " 'Death by Boiling Hot Tar. You are tied to a tree while a pot six times larger than a spaghetti pot—' "

"Jump to the next one." Violet was getting impatient.

"Oh, okay," said Melissa. " 'Number 51. Death by Inquo, the terrible itching mosquito of Tibet.' "

"Too hard to come by," said Violet. "Next."

" 'Death from Not Looking Where You're Going.' "

"Nah."

" 'Death by tickling.' "

There was a long pause. Finally Violet asked, "How many youngers have been tickled by their olders?"

"Me!" They all shouted and raised their hands.

Another long pause. "This is it, then," said Violet. "*This* is perfect."

Simon began gasping, tiny, pathetic little gasps like he was trying to catch his breath but couldn't. No one paid any attention.

"Should I read on? There's a whole paragraph," said Melissa.

"We'll save it until later. For now, let the prisoner imagine what it says."

"Ooh, that is so mean," Melissa said admiringly.

"Cool," said Cynthia.

"Attention," said Violet, snapping her shoulders back and clicking her heels.

All the youngers scrambled up and saluted.

"I, General Violet Sparks, hereby declare that the prisoner, Simon Sparks, is sentenced to death by tickling. Tickling will commence at exactly 11:05 A.M. Simon Sparks will laugh himself into the grave by 11:32 unless . . . " She didn't finish.

"Unless wha-a-a-t?" Simon could barely squeak it out.

"Never mind," said Violet.

CHAPTER THIRTEEN

In which Alfred is one radical parrot, and Claire Sparks freaks out

The next morning, Artie dragged himself into the kitchen. He was barely able to put one foot in front of the other. "Waffles marinara," trilled Antonia Box, putting out a big platter of waffles in strawberry sauce.

"I'm not hungry," said Artie.

"Nonsense."

Artie sat down, put his head on his plate, and closed his eyes. He didn't even look when he heard Gabriel walk in.

"Gabriel, my morning glory, Arturo's acting like he's not hungry, but I'm sure when he sees *you* eat . . . "

Right, Mom, thought Artie. I'll eat like him, talk like him, walk like him—

"I cannot eat a bite, don't make me," said Gabriel.

"Huh?" Artie perked up.

"I had a terrible nightmare." Artie opened his eyes and peeked over to see Gabriel slouched in his chair, his face so pale his freckles stood out like measles.

"It wasn't a picture dream, just sounds." Gabriel put his hands over his ears as if the sounds still haunted him. "This voice—"

"Whose voice?"

"Nobody we know, I assure you. This voice was saying over and over, 'Just like Arturo, just like Arturo.'" Gabriel pointed at Artie. "It was telling me to be like him."

Artie sat up. He'd forgotten—he'd forgotten Alfred!

"This sounds very significant." Antonia Box sat down and began drumming her fingers on the table. She got a very serious look on her face, like a world problem had just been presented to her and she had to solve it. "Maybe it was God whispering in your ear. Or maybe . . . maybe it was your great grandfather from Sicily, speaking from the grave."

"My great grandfather gave me a horrible headache," said Gabriel.

"Don't insult dear Federico, my father's father," said Antonia.

"Yeah," said Artie, who was suddenly starving and shoveled a big bite of waffle into his mouth. "*De-*

lizioso, my dear mama." He bounced over and gave her a big kiss. "Isn't it a fabulous day?" He ran down the hall, whipped into Gabriel's room, and opened the closet. "Alfred, my pal."

"Just like Arturo," said Alfred.

"You said it!" Artie scooped up Alfred. He ran back down the hall and out the front door. "Be back later," he shouted.

Before he was down the front walk, Alfred squawked once more, "Just like Arturo."

Gabriel screamed, "I heard it again."

"So did I," said Antonia Box, amazed. "It's a sign. It's Federico for sure." She called up to the ceiling, "We hear you, Federico." Then she said to Gabriel, "This means you should start listening to rocking and rolling tapes just like . . . "

"Don't say it, don't say it, DON'T SAY IT," shrieked Gabriel. But Antonia Box said it anyway— "Arturo." She rolled the *r*'s over her tongue and savored them as if they were melted mozzarella.

Artie danced down the block. He skipped. He jumped.

"Artie."

He slid to a stop, holding Alfred in his arms. It was Claire Sparks. "Have you seen Violet?"

"No."

"What about Simon?"

"No."

"Oh, dear." Mrs. Sparks kept squeezing her hands together as if she were hoping some information might drop out. "They weren't in their rooms this morning. Do you suppose they got up early?"

"I don't know," said Artie, crossing his fingers under Alfred's feathers where they couldn't be seen.

"Well, if you see them, tell them to come home. If they don't show up soon, I'm going to have to call the police."

"Oh, wait," said Artie. He was so excited he'd forgotten Violet's orders. "Violet told me to tell you to look in the refrigerator."

"Look in the refrigerator? For what?" asked Claire Sparks.

Artie shrugged.

"Excuse me. Hello." Mrs. Ruggles was waving and running toward them in her bathrobe and slippers. "Cynthia's missing."

"I'll be seeing you," said Artie.

He sped off as three front doors opened on the block. "Have you seen Christopher?" yelled Christopher's mom. "Where's Denise?" her mom shouted. Then Artie heard Melissa's dad calling, "Melissa? Melissa?"

"Look in Violet's refrigerator," shouted Artie. He

ducked under a bush, cut through an alley, and was gone.

He almost flew past the center on his way to the wild when he caught sight of a patch of red. He braked, scorching his sneakers.

"Davy, is that you?" He went around the tennis courts to the bleachers just as Violet appeared.

"Is it safe for you to be out?" he asked Violet.

"A soldier is in trouble," said Violet. She tipped the fire helmet up and looked under it. "Hello, Davy."

"Hi, Davy, my savior, my pal, my best buddy," said Artie.

"Huh?" said Davy.

"Just like Arturo," said Alfred.

Davy stared, flabbergasted. "Alfred, you did it."

"No, you did," said Violet.

"You're brilliant, a genius," said Artie.

Alfred flew out of Artie's arms and back where he belonged, on top of Davy's helmet. As soon as he had preened a bit, he leaned over and kissed Davy on the nose.

Violet looked from Davy to Artie. "You know what?" she said. "You guys don't need me."

"We don't?" asked Artie.

"I'll see you later at the hideout." She made a smart sharp turn, and left.

Artie sat down next to Davy on the bleachers. "So, best buddy, tell me all about it."

"I swallowed a lizard," said Davy. He blurted out the story.

"And now your sister's happier than ever?"

"Yeah. She'll always get me. It's stupid of me even to try."

"That's the way I felt about Gabriel until you helped me. So now I'm going to help you. Let's go. It's you, me, and Alfred. Two brave musketeers and one radical parrot." He dragged Davy up. "Watch out, Margaret. Hip, hip, hurrah."

"Hip, hip, hurrah," said Davy.

"Louder," said Artie.

"Hip, hip, hurrah," they shouted together.

"Are you really my best friend?" said Davy.

"You bet," said Artie.

"That's my favorite part." Davy straightened his helmet. "Charge," he said.

"Which direction?" said Artie.

Davy pointed to the center. "Thataway."

Claire Sparks opened the refrigerator. "I wonder what I'm looking for?" she asked no one in particular, although Melissa's mom and dad and a couple of other parents were gathered in her kitchen, waiting to find out. "I love surprises, don't you?"

"No," said Cynthia Ruggles's mom. "I hate them. And, speaking of surprises, I found the most peculiar contraptions in Cynthia's bedroom. Cages of some sort."

"Bird cages?" asked Claire Sparks, looking on the top shelf, behind the milk and the mayonnaise.

"No."

"What was in them?" She checked under the American cheese, then opened the crisper.

"Nothing. But something had been, because there were droppings everywhere."

"This must be it." Claire Sparks held up a tape cassette. "It was under the lettuce."

They all followed her into the living room and over to the stereo. "Oh, dear," she said, looking at all the dials and buttons. "I wish Simon were here. He's the best at working this."

"Hurry, please," said Mrs. Ruggles, yawning. "I'm beat. Bobby found a lizard in his bed last night. He practically had a fit."

"So did my Matthew," said another mom.

"And my Jeffrey," said another.

"My Suzette's a basket case," said Mrs. McFree.

All the parents stared at one another.

Claire Sparks closed the instruction booklet and pushed a button. The cassette player slid out. She popped in the tape, then sat down and waited. They all waited.

There were some weird sounds. Then a voice said, "Is it working?"

"Who's that?" asked Claire Sparks.

"Shush," said everyone else.

"This is General Violet Sparks."

"A general? My Violet?"

"Shush!" Everyone leaned closer to the stereo as Violet's voice, faint but firm, was heard.

"This is an official announcement. All the younger brothers and sisters in Mountain Terrace have declared war on the older brothers and sisters."

"Oh, sure," said Mr. McFree sarcastically.

"We are using their own weapons against them so they'll know what it feels like. We have taken our first prisoner, my revolting brother, Simon."

Claire Sparks gripped the arms of her chair.

"And unless the olders take back everything they have ever done to their youngers, and change their disgusting older ways for good, he's done for." There was a click, and the tape switched off.

"It's a joke, it's just a joke," said Mr. McFree. "You know kids. They're playing a game."

"Violet doesn't joke," said Claire Sparks. "I wish

she did." She got up, took a few steps toward the kitchen, stopped, and turned the other way. She was acting dizzy, as if she'd just been punched.

"Why don't you sit down?" said Mrs. McFree, helping her back to her chair.

"Well, fortunately, whatever's going on, my little princess isn't involved," said Mr. McFree. "Melissa wouldn't hurt a fly."

"Wise up," said Cynthia's mom. "They're all involved. Cynthia's going to be grounded for a month. Maybe a year."

"If you can find her," said Mr. McFree.

Claire Sparks stared numbly at the stereo. "Simon can work that. He can always figure things like that out without even looking in the instruction book. What did Violet mean—'he's done for'?"

CHAPTER FOURTEEN

In which Davy shouts "Duh," Margaret circles the room in a dither, and the parents rant

Artie and Davy, with Alfred perched on his helmet, peeked in the window of the community center. They watched Davy's sister, in a lavender tutu, perform her dying swan bow, where her head touched one knee while the other leg shot out behind her. "She's going to be mean," said Davy.

"So what?" said Artie.

"You're right—so what! Let's get her."

They circled around to the front and into the dance studio.

"Greetings, Arturo Xavier Box." Margaret did a pirouette. "I see you're hanging out with Parrot Head."

"Don't call me that," said Davy. Their eyes locked.

It was an eye-wrestling match: Whose stare could wither the other's? Margaret's beady eyes bore into his. Davy's eyelids got heavier and heavier and heavier.

"When in doubt," Artie whispered.

"Duh." Thanks to Violet's training, the word popped out of Davy's mouth automatically.

Margaret blinked. Artie jabbed Davy in the ribs— "Way to go!"

Margaret tossed her head. "I can recite six ballet terms—entrechat, plié, pirouette, pied-à-terre, pas de deux, and mal à la tête. Davy doesn't know a plié from a pretzel."

"Duh," said Davy and Artie together.

"I have perfect posture like a great ballerina and Davy walks like the hunchback of Notre Dame."

"Duh," they shouted.

"Stop it." Margaret put her hands over her ears.

"Duh," they said.

"Stop it. I hate it."

"Duh."

"I hate you."

"Duh, duh, duh, duh, duh."

Alfred flew off Davy's helmet and landed on Margaret's head. "Yikes," she screamed. She waved her arms wildly, trying to knock him off.

"Duh," said Alfred, staying put.

"He's learned another word," said Davy, amazed.

Margaret was running in circles. "Get it off. Help!"

Alfred's claws were firmly planted in her thick red hair. "Duh, duh, duh," said Alfred.

"Let's get out of here." Artie grabbed Davy's arm. He pulled Davy out of the room while Margaret was still going 'round and 'round like a tape machine on fast-forward. He and Davy raced out of the community center, then stopped short.

"Well, rock me and roll me," said Artie. "Look who's coming."

"It's everyone's parents," said Davy, "and they've got, uh-oh, they've got the olders!"

Artie grabbed Davy's hand and they took off. Jumping over rocks, dodging tumbleweeds, they sped to the hideout in the wild.

The parents herded their older children into the center. Mrs. Ruggles nudged Bobby forward, but every time she looked away, he veered toward home. "He's a complete wreck," said Mrs. Ruggles. "Has been ever since that lizard."

Gabriel walked with his hands over his ears. "Do you realize your father couldn't go to the deli because of this?" said Antonia Box. "I don't see why you're being so difficult. Arturo was just like you for ages, so now it's your turn to be like him." Gabriel sat down on the sidewalk and wouldn't budge. His parents picked him up. "He weighs more than lead linguine," said his mom as they lugged him into room 101 of the community center and deposited him on a chair.

Suzette wore a veil and her turban so no one could see her blotchy, red face and very short hair. She walked docilely behind her parents.

Claire Sparks stood in front of the microphone. "Please sit down. Please, hurry, please.

"We have a problem," she said.

"Thanks to you," a parent yelled.

Claire Sparks gulped. "I think," she said hesitantly, "I think it doesn't help to blame. It's hard being a younger."

"That's true." Mr. McFree stood up. "I was a younger brother, and my older brother used to tell me to hit him. I'd do it, and he'd tell on me."

"Well, I'm an older sister," said Mrs. McFree, "and once my little sister was born, no one paid me any attention. Besides, you're always on Melissa's side."

"Please, please, this isn't helping," said Claire Sparks. "We have to find out what is really happening to—"

The door burst open. Everyone swung around as Margaret Brown ran in, howling. Alfred was still sitting on her head. He was more adept at staying put than a cowboy on a bronco. "Duh, duh, duh, duh," he squawked.

Margaret circled the room in a dither. She slid to a stop right next to Claire Sparks and said, "I'm Margaret Alice Brown, the smartest person in Mountain Terrace, and my brother is the—" She didn't finish the sentence. She crumpled to the floor like a rag doll.

Mrs. Brown rushed onto the stage, waving her arms. "Get off my daughter, you hideous bird." Alfred flew into the air. Hovering over the parents and olders, he let out a final, deafening "duh." Everyone froze, stunned and frightened, as if they had been given both a threat and a warning. Alfred flew out the window.

"Who did this to you, Maggiekins?" said Mrs. Brown, cradling Margaret's head.

Margaret's eyes fluttered, "Davy."

"Oh, dear. It's definitely happening," said Claire Sparks. Her mouth trembled, her lower lip jutted forward, making a sad little shelf. "I think the older brothers and sisters had better do what Violet said, and take it back."

"What does 'take it back' mean?" asked a parent.

"Apologize."

"Apologize for what?"

"They know," said Claire Sparks. "Believe me."

"Take it back. Take it back, or else." There was pandemonium as parents hammered at their kids. "Take it back, or no more TV, no more dessert, no more nothing." Only Mr. McFree sat there with his mouth clamped shut.

"What is it?" Mrs. McFree asked.

"I think we should butt out."

"You're right."

"What did you say?"

"I agreed with you," she said, smiling.

Mr. McFree grabbed his wife's hand. "Excuse us, Suzette."

They made their way to the front of the room, through all the ranting parents. Claire Sparks stepped aside to let them speak. Mr. McFree tapped the mike a few times, making a weird echoing sound. "Hello," he said loudly. "May we have your attention? We have an idea."

"A very good idea that we agree on." Mrs. McFree leaned over and shyly gave her husband a kiss on the cheek.

"We should butt out," said Mr. McFree.

"What?" said Claire Sparks.

"It doesn't help kids when you interfere," said Mrs. McFree. "They have to work it out for them-selves."

"But suppose something happens to Simon? Suppose Violet hurts him or—" She couldn't finish the sentence.

"We have to trust our kids," said Mr. McFree. "It's the only way to restore harmony."

All the parents looked at their kids. No one said anything for a minute. Then Mrs. Ruggles said, "Bye, Bobby, I'm outta here." Antonia Box raised her eyes to the ceiling. "Great grandfather Federico, don't flip a gasket, but we're going down to the deli to have meatball heros."

One by one and two by two the parents all left. The McFrees walked out slowly, holding hands. "Harmony would be a very nice name for our baby," said Mr. McFree. "What do you think?"

"I love it," said Mrs. McFree.

"You do?"

"It's completely divine." She kissed him again.

Claire Sparks was the last to go. As she walked out, she looked at each older, begging with her eyes, Remember Simon, remember Violet. At the door, she stopped and turned. "I'm trusting you." She said it like a threat: Take *that*! Not one older brother or sister even turned to look.

CHAPTER FIFTEEN

In which Violet rewards valor, and Davy makes a speech

Artie and Davy raced into the hideout. "Margaret flipped," whooped Artie.

"Went bonkers," shouted Davy.

All the youngers gathered around as Davy ran in circles, imitating Margaret, shrieking in a high-pitched voice, and trying to knock an imaginary bird off his head.

"Well done," said Violet.

Davy stopped running. His face was flushed with excitement.

"I have to admit something, Davy," said Melissa. "I didn't want you in our army, but I was wrong."

"That's okay," said Davy.

"I really like you, and I admire you."

"You do?" Two big tears welled up in Davy's eyes. No one had ever admired him before. He wiped his eyes quickly with his arm, doing it sort of casually, as if he just had a sweaty brow or something.

Artie winked at him as if to say, I know what's going on, best buddy, but I won't give you away.

There was a strange whirring sound, flapping . . . the leaves rustled. Everyone looked up.

"That's my Alfred," yelled Davy.

Alfred zoomed down, landing on his favorite perch, Davy's helmet. "Duh," said Alfred.

"Attention, everyone," said Violet. "I, General Violet Sparks, am going to present two commendations for exceptional valor in the field of duty.

"To Davy Brown, most improved soldier." Davy stood tall. He tipped his helmet back so he could look Violet in the eye. Violet saluted, then shook his hand and gave him a Y carved out of wood.

"I made it with my tools," said Melissa. "You can use it for a paperweight."

"Could I say something?" Davy asked.

"Permission granted," said Violet.

"I think . . . ," Davy took a deep breath, "I think this is the best day of my life. I found a best friend. Also, I did my sister in, and got an award. It's all because you believed in me, Violet."

All the youngers cheered, not just for Davy but for Violet, the greatest general of all.

"And I would also like to give a special award for smarts and imagination to Alfred," said Violet.

"Duh," said Alfred.

The youngers cheered, Mugs barked, and Ivy meowed.

"What's next?" said Davy.

Silence. Violet turned toward the pit.

CHAPTER SIXTEEN

In which the olders cross their fingers and try to keep them crossed

Inside the community center, Margaret Brown was still flat on the floor, too exhausted to sit up. Suzette McFree was mumbling under her veil, "Not my fault," but it came out, "Noma faul." Other olders held their heads—their ears were ringing from their parents' rants and ravings.

Bobby Ruggles looked around. Someone had to do something. Someone had to take charge. He got up, not too steadily. He scratched his arm, then his leg—Was something still crawling on him?—then, slowly, he made his way to the microphone.

"Uh, hi." Bobby's voice cracked. He looked nervous. "I feel weird," said Bobby.

No response, except some scratching and Suzette mumbling, "Noma faul."

"You're supposed to say, 'How weird?' " said Bobby.

Still no response.

"Uh, okay, never mind. Look, those youngers say we're supposed to take it back, but I say we never did anything."

A few olders sat up straighter and stopped mid-scratch.

"And I don't believe that stuff about Simon," said Bobby. "He's too smart to be kidnapped by a bunch of boneheads."

Suzette stood up. It was sudden and startling, as if someone had flipped open the top of a jack-in-the-box and Suzette had shot out. "Melissa made Jock hate me. She should take it back, not me. And now I can't even toss my hair because it's too short. Tossing is my favorite thing." She burst into tears. She mushed the veil against her face to wipe them.

"We never did anything to them," said Bobby.

"Yeah!" Now everyone was shouting.

"We won't take it back."

"Yeah!" everyone shouted.

"I will."

"Huh?" said Bobby.

"I will." Gabriel waved his hand.

"Shut up," an older yelled.

"Let him speak," said another.

The olders started quarreling as Gabriel walked to the front, ignoring the insults. Bobby gave him a dirty look, but stepped aside to let him have the mike.

"Dear friends and olders . . . "

Everyone groaned.

"I feel it is my duty to confess," said Gabriel. "I tried to be good all the time just to bug Artie. Once I even kissed my mother's hand to make him throw up. I pretended to hate rock 'n' roll so my parents would make him stop listening to it."

"Way to go," shouted an older. Everyone cheered.

"But I was mean. We all were."

"Boo! Get off the stage! Who cares?"

Gabriel shouted to be heard. "When my parents told Artie to be like me, I was especially glad because I knew it made Artie miserable, and now they're telling me to be like him and I . . . " Gabriel had to stop, there was too much hissing.

Margaret Brown sat up. "I'm the smartest person here and I say get rid of the traitor."

A bunch of olders rushed at Gabriel, knocked him down, and started pulling him feet first out of the room. As they dragged him up the aisle, he shouted, "If Simon was kidnapped and you don't take it back, he'll die. How will you feel then?"

Silence, except for a thud as the olders dropped his feet.

"I'd feel bad," said Bobby finally, wondering if Simon really could have been kidnapped. He guessed it was possible.

"We could take it back and not really mean it," said Margaret. "We could keep our fingers crossed."

"True," said Bobby.

"See what I mean about how smart I am?" said Margaret.

"Let's vote on it," shouted an older.

"Okay," said Bobby. "All those in favor of taking it back just to save Simon but not really meaning it raise your hand."

They all raised their hands, except Gabriel.

"All opposed?"

Gabriel raised his hand.

"Hey, I thought you wanted this," said Bobby.

"We have to mean it," said Gabriel.

"No way," shouted the rest of the olders.

"Well," said Bobby, "majority rules. Cross your fingers. Let's get it over with."

The olders started talking to themselves. As they did, they stood up and began to fan out, moving out of room 101, into the hall, and then onto the lawn. Parents gathered and watched.

"I take it back," said Bobby, "that I pulled the head off Cynthia's doll, and pushed its eyes in." He talked in a singsong, as if he barely knew what he was saying, and nodded to the rhythm. " . . . that, when Cynthia was a baby"—nod—"I dropped her on the floor"—nod—"and said she fell."

"Well," Suzette was saying at the same time. "I take it back that I said Melissa wasn't the princess type, even though it's true." Suzette smiled a grand smile—a sort of queen-being-kind-to-the-poor-peasant kind of smile. "I take it back that I told her red paint was freckle-removing cream." Suzette's smile faded.

She remembered how sad Melissa had looked when she tried to toss her hair and it had just lain there. She thought of all the times Melissa had washed the dishes even though it was Suzette's turn, because Suzette had wanted to talk to Jock. It must be hard, Suzette thought, to have a sister as stupendously pretty and popular as I am. "Melissa," she called. "Melissa, wherever you are, if you're listening, I take it all back."

"She means it," said Max, who was watching from the sidelines with his parents and Violet's mom.

"Yes, she does," said Mrs. McFree.

"I'm so glad," said Claire Sparks, "now my Simon will be fine."

"Maybe not," said Max, watching Margaret Brown.

"I take it back that I said Davy was a dope. Did you know dope rhymes with *mope, rope, cope,* and *soap?* I can rhyme and Davy can't even do opposites."

"Get a load of that," said Mr. McFree. "She's taking back one and adding one at the same time. Oops— wait a minute, hold it."

Margaret got a funny look on her face. "It also rhymes with *hope,*" she said, remembering the look on Davy's face when he peeked out from underneath his fire helmet the time she told him she would give him something nice that rhymed with *rug.* He was expecting a hug and got a potato bug.

"She means it now," said Max emphatically.

"Thank goodness," said Claire Sparks.

"Davy," wailed Margaret, "Please forgive me. I vow to change my ways."

"Uh-oh." Claire Sparks clutched her hands to her heart.

"What's wrong now?" said Mrs. McFree.

"Suppose Violet doesn't know? Suppose all these olders are taking it back, and she doesn't know, so she does something to Simon anyway?" Claire Sparks started gasping.

"Keep calm," said Mrs. McFree.

"I can't, I just can't."

"Hey—maybe Max knows where the younger kids are. Max?"

No answer.

Mrs. McFree looked around. "Where did Max go?" she asked her husband.

"Max?" he called. "Hey, has anyone seen Max?"

CHAPTER SEVENTEEN

In which General Violet Sparks tastes it, embraces it, rolls around, wallows in it, and wails

Violet stood at the edge of the pit. She stared down at Simon. He wasn't a brother. He wasn't even a human being. He was a wart, a mutant. She was doing all mankind a favor by ridding the universe of him. She imagined that she wasn't just a general, she was a general descended from a great Greek warrior, and all the Greek gods on clouds above were bowing in gratitude, just as they had to her noble ancestor.

The youngers stood smartly—all lined up around the pit with long branches over their shoulders. Ticklers, Violet called them. The youngers held them like rifles, except Melissa. She had Cynthia's book.

"Does the prisoner have any last words?" asked Violet.

"Blubba, blubba, blubba," said Simon, who was

lying face down. He was trying to say, "I'm sorry, I take everything back," but was so terrified that the words wouldn't come out.

"Blubba? That's it?"

The youngers giggled.

"Attention," snapped Violet. They stopped immediately.

"Let it be recorded for history that the prisoner went to his death without taking anything back."

There followed a moment of silence. Violet stood at her fanciest, shoulders back, chin up. Then, "Is my henchman ready?" she asked.

Melissa nodded and opened the book to page 135. The youngers moved their ticklers off their shoulders and held them in front.

"Now aim," said Violet. Melissa held the book up and cleared her throat. The youngers pointed their ticklers at Simon.

"Read!" she snapped.

" 'Death by Tickling,' " read Melissa. Her voice was loud. It was confident. " 'This is in three stages.' Do you hear?" She peered down into the pit. Her eyes narrowed as she viewed the victim. I'm Violet's henchman, she reminded herself. Although she wasn't absolutely sure what that meant, she knew it was someone loyal and fierce. " 'Stage one, a million feathers descend on your bare feet.' " She imagined

that each word was an arrow aimed at Simon's heart.
" 'And, even though you are scared dumb, you can't help laughing.' "

"Oh, oh, oh," said Simon. He started giggling.

"It's working. Great," said Melissa. She continued reading. " 'Then, while you are giggling helplessly, a bunch of other ticklers get to work on your knees.' "

"Hee-hee-hee-hee-hee-hee-hee-hee," giggled Simon as the ticklers began working the backs of his knees, on that little crease where the thigh meets the calf.

Violet put her hands over her ears. She'd forgotten that Simon had the dumbest laugh.

" 'Your hee-hees are getting louder,' " read Melissa. " 'They are turning into ha-has, then haw-haw-haws.' "

Right on schedule, Simon started ha-haing, then hawing. He sounded like a donkey in hysterics.

"Do stage two," said Violet urgently. She couldn't wait. Finally Simon was in her power, utterly and forever.

" 'Stage two,' " shouted Melissa. " 'Under your arms.' "

The ticklers moved to Simon's armpits. " 'Your haws are turning into yuks.' "

"Yuka-yuka-yuka." Simon rolled around, trying to escape the ticklers, but one was waiting for him everywhere he rolled. Violet didn't blink. She didn't want to miss a split second of his agony. "Go on," she said to Melissa. "Hurry up."

" 'Now for the super-duper tickler part.' "

Youngers moved to make room for a girl dressed in black and wearing a skeleton mask. "It's Cynthia," Artie whispered to Davy. He remembered her mask from Halloween.

Cynthia carried a long pole with a pliers attached to the end. She aimed it at Simon's knees: squeeze, squeeze, squeeze.

Melissa read on, whipping the words out. " 'Your laughs can't be heard now. You are laughing so loud no sound comes out.' " Simon was suddenly silent, although his body rolled around and his stomach bounced up and down as if someone were using it for a trampoline. All the youngers were silent, stunned by the strange sight. " 'This is where the laughter stops being funny and turns to poison.' "

"Yes," shouted Violet.

" 'The final stage,' " read Melissa. She paused, then hissed, "*This* is curtains."

" 'Lissa?"

"Huh?" said Melissa.

"Go on, hurry," said Violet.

"Melissa, it's me." Max tugged on her T-shirt. "I knew I'd find you," he said proudly.

"I'm busy, get lost," said Melissa.

"But I have to tell you something, something important. Something great about the olders."

"Butt out, okay?"

"But Melissa—"

"Squelch it, shrimp. Just squelch it! Oh my gosh. OH MY GOSH!" Melissa slammed the book closed.

"Continue," ordered Violet.

"I can't," said Melissa.

"Take him prisoner," barked Violet.

"No!" Melissa grabbed Max and held him close. "Violet, don't you see? I said, 'Squelch it, shrimp.' Just like Suzette."

"Who cares? Get on with it."

"But I did it, Violet. I did it, too."

"Did what?" Violet's face twisted into an angry rage. How dare Melissa mess everything up now?

"I acted like an older. I am an older! I knew it, but I forgot, because I'm in the middle." Melissa slapped her hands to her cheeks, startled, as if she'd just discovered Alaska but had been standing on it her whole life.

"Melissa, you can take back what you said to me," said Max. "They're all taking it back."

"I take it back." Melissa gave Max a hug. "Did you hear that, Violet? They're all taking it back. The war is over. We won."

"It's not over," said Violet. She grabbed the book and frantically thumbed though it. "Attention," she shouted. All the youngers, except Melissa, snapped their shoulders back, clicked their heels, and saluted. Violet's hand stopped with a slap on page 136. Her face was white, except for two red circles of thrill on each cheek. There was perspiration on her forehead, and the curls of her hair spiked.

She looked into the pit. Simon's stomach heaved worse than ever, the ripples now whipped up through his chest. She began to read.

" 'Stage three begins with tickling behind the ears.' " Violet's voice was mechanical and cold as Arctic ice. The youngers tickled, following her instructions with trance-like precision.

Melissa held Max tight and pressed his head against her, so he couldn't see into the pit. If he even glimpsed what was going on, she was sure he would have nightmares and never forget.

" 'This ear-tickling makes your neck wiggle so the poison spreads to the brain,' " said Violet. Her body became so rigid it almost vibrated as the youngers obediently tickled. Stop, stop, Melissa silently begged. Ripples went through Simon's cheeks, his eyes bulged. " 'It's almost over now,' " read Violet, " 'and it's a welcome relief.' " Simon's whole face pulsated.

" 'One, two, three, done.' " Violet dropped the book, and stared as Simon's face stopped throbbing, as his quivering, twitching body switched off.

"Oh, Violet, no," moaned Melissa.

"Hush," hissed Violet. She wanted to savor the moment. She wanted to taste it, embrace it, roll around and wallow in it. Simon was finally, once and for all, gone. Out of her life. Finished. He would never torture her again.

"NOOOOOOOOOOOOOOOOOO!" Violet let out a gigantic wail. It was so loud and so surprising that even Violet didn't know where it came from. She looked around in confusion, then realized the wail was hers. "Simon, no!" The words ripped out of her. Did she really speak them? Was that her voice? She threw herself into the pit.

Melissa let go of Max, who almost fell in himself when he saw Violet down there. All the youngers stopped being soldiers and started screaming. It was as if they had gotten on a roller coaster and discovered right in the middle of the ride that it was just too scary for them.

"Simon, come back, don't die. Simon, please." Violet was crying and kissing her brother. She'd never kissed him before, at least not that she could remember, and now she couldn't stop. "Oh, please come back, please. I love you." Violet sat back on her heels and let the tears roll down her cheeks. There was no sign, no breath, no twitch that he was alive. "I forgive you, so forgive me," said Violet. "Tell me it's not too late."

"I hear you," shouted Melissa. "And maybe Simon does, too, wherever he is."

Simon's eyes fluttered. "Look, he blinked, he blinked," screamed Melissa. Violet's eyes were so blurry from tears that she couldn't see. "Are you there?" said Violet. "Are you back?"

"I love you, too," said Simon. "But don't tell Bobby."

"Bobby took everything back," shouted Max. "He was practically the first."

Violet frantically untied her brother, then collapsed next to him. "You were so mean to me. Over and over and over again. It really hurt."

"I'm sorry. I really am sorry."

"He means it," Max whispered to Melissa.

"Will you change your disgusting older ways?" asked Violet.

"I swear it," said Simon.

"Hit it, Artie," shouted Violet.

The youngers moved apart to make room for Artie, who sauntered up as if he had been performing for years. He flipped a curl over his forehead. "Introducing the great Artie Box," said Davy. "Duh," said Alfred. Artie sang with all his heart:

> *We had strength, and we had courage,*
> *So all the youngers changed the world.*
> *We fought the olders,*
> *We had fun.*
> *We fought the olders, aaand*
> *We won!*

"All together now," he shouted.

Davy took Artie's hand, and Artie took Melissa's, and Melissa took Max's, and Max took Cynthia's, and on and on around the pit. "We had strength, and we had courage," they sang.

Violet and Simon stood up and put their arms around each other. Violet, who'd never sung the song before even though she was the force behind it, joined in. Simon did, too. "So all the youngers changed the world."

Their voices carried out of the wild to the community center. "Do you hear that?" Claire Sparks gave a joyful shout. "That's Violet and Simon. Everything's okay. That's my children!"

Kids and parents all through Mountain Terrace stuck their heads out of windows and sang along.

Antonia and Antonio Box put down their meatball heros, opened the door to the deli, and joined in. Suzette, Margaret, Bobby, and Gabriel sang loudest of all.

"I bet my brother wrote that," said Gabriel proudly.

"We won, we won, we won, we won." The song ended with the youngers chanting softer and softer until the song faded out.

"Good grief, how are we going to get out of here?" said Violet, suddenly realizing that she and Simon were stuck in the pit.

"No problem," said Melissa. "Where's my tool kit?"

"Over here," said Cynthia, who was about to put back the pliers that she had used for the knee-squeezer.

"Everyone hand over their ticklers," shouted Melissa.

Using screws and nuts, Melissa quickly fastened the branches together to make a ladder. "It's rickety," she said, "so come up one at a time."

"Thanks," said Violet.

"Aye, aye, General," said Melissa.

"After you," said Simon. He offered Violet his hand.